'I can assure you, we are who we say we are,' Maximillian told him.

'I believe ᴧ,' the elemental replied, 'for it is well known th   however much he changes his appearanc' the Ugly One can always be told by a ring with c   ꜱen stone upon it that he cannot conceal. That is wʰ   ꜱsked to see your hands. Now perhaps you woulꜱ   e to take some tea with me?'

'We reᴀ   have to go…' Maximillian began.

'You reⱼ. ꜱ my hospitality?' the elemental snarled menacingly.

'We'd love some tea,' Otto declared, 'wouldn't we?'

'Can't think of anything nicer,' Juliet agreed.

ORCHARD BOOKS
338 Euston Road, London NW1 3BH
Orchard Books Australia
Level 17/207 Kent Street, Sydney, NSW 2000

First published in 2011 by Orchard Books

A Paperback Original

ISBN 978 1 40830 682 6

A CIP catalogue record for this book is available from the
British Library.

1 3 5 7 9 10 8 6 4 2

Printed in Great Britain

Orchard Books is a division of Hachette Children's Books,
an Hachette UK company.

www.hachette.co.uk

THE MAGICAL DETECTIVES

BRIAN KEANEY

ORCHARD BOOKS

CONTENTS

A NOTE TO THE READER

In the first *Magical Detectives* book, Otto Spinoza, who lives with his mother above a second-hand bookshop in the sleepy little town of Bridlington Chawley, met Maximillian Hawksmoor, a magician and a detective.

Together with Juliet Pennington, a girl in Otto's class at school, and Cornelius, her cat, Otto and Max travelled to a world very different from their own. This world is called Quillipoth and it is inhabited by magical beings called elementals.

In the course of this adventure, Otto learned that the people he had always thought of as his parents were really his step-parents, that he had been born a hundred and fifty years earlier and brought to our time through a magical portal, and that he was descended from Balshazzar, the ruler of Ancient Babylon.

Two other remarkable things resulted from

that trip to Quillipoth. One was that Cornelius began to talk just like a human being. The other was that Otto, Juliet and Cornelius agreed to join Maximillian Hawksmoor's Magical Detective Agency.

1

MADAME SIKURSKY

'What I don't understand is why Madame Sikursky is performing in Bridlington Chawley,' said Otto Spinoza. He was twelve years old with floppy brown hair and clear blue eyes, and would have looked to most passers-by like a perfectly ordinary schoolboy. Only a handful of people knew that in his spare time he was a magical detective, dedicated to solving crimes with a supernatural origin.

'I don't think it's particularly strange,' said Juliet Pennington, Otto's friend and fellow detective. 'Madame Sikursky is a stage hypnotist. Giving performances is what she does.'

Juliet, who was a few weeks older than Otto, was a very sensible girl, not at all the sort of person you would expect to be involved in supernatural happenings. But she'd been accidentally caught up in a magical adventure with Otto the previous summer and found to her surprise that she enjoyed it enormously. Now she was staying with Otto for a few weeks because her parents had gone to Cheshire to look after her grandmother.

The pair of them were standing outside the Belsham Theatre in Bridlington Chawley at seven o'clock on a rather damp November evening. They were waiting for Maximillian Hawksmoor, the founder of the Magical Detective agency to which they all belonged. He was the one who had bought them tickets to see the world-famous hypnotist.

'Yes, but she's been on TV,' Otto pointed out. 'She's appeared in London, Paris, New York, Rome and now...here. It doesn't make sense. I mean Bridlington Chawley isn't exactly the showbiz capital of the world, is it?'

'Here's Max now,' Juliet said. 'Why don't you ask him?'

Striding briskly along the street was a tall man with jet black hair, very bushy eyebrows and a hooked nose that made him look a little like a bird of prey. He smiled when he saw Otto and Juliet. 'All ready for an evening's entertainment?' he asked.

'Yes – but what's going on, Max?' Otto asked. 'How come Madame Sikursky is performing in Bridlington Chawley, of all places?'

Maximillian shrugged his shoulders. 'It's a mystery,' he said. 'But mysteries are what we specialise in, right?'

'True,' Otto agreed.

'So let's go inside and see if we can solve it.'

The Belsham Theatre was already packed as the trio made their way towards their seats. Everyone was obviously looking forward to the show and a buzz of eager conversation filled the auditorium.

Everyone except Juliet. 'I'm not sure about hypnotists,' she said when they were sitting down at last.

'What do you mean you're not sure about them?' Otto asked.

'Well, I've seen one on TV who made people believe that their seats were red hot and stuff like that, but I think it was all fake.'

'Why?'

'I just think there are some people who will

do anything to be the centre of attention and when the hypnotist asks for volunteers, they're always the ones who go up on stage. Then when they're up there, they just play along because everyone is looking at them.'

A few moments later the curtain came up, and the audience began clapping enthusiastically as a striking-looking woman in a long black dress walked onto the stage. She was nearly six feet tall, with shoulder-length dark hair, high cheekbones, and a very white face in which her lipsticked mouth stood out like a red gash.

'She looks like someone from a vampire movie,' Juliet whispered.

'Ladies and gentlemen,' Madame Sikursky began, speaking with a heavy foreign accent, 'tonight I am going to show you the power of *true* hypnotism. There will be no tricks, no stunts, no cheap laughs. Just a demonstration of the hidden powers of the mind. Powers that we all possess but which in most people are buried so far below the surface that they never learn to use them.'

From the moment she opened her mouth it seemed to Otto that there was something compelling about Madame Sikursky. Her voice drew him in; he felt as though he was listening not to a woman talking into a microphone on a stage, but to a voice inside his head.

'Most of you gathered here tonight probably think that your life started on the day you were born,' Madame Sikursky continued. 'You assume that you cannot possibly have experience of anything that took place before that day, except perhaps by reading about it in history books. But you would be wrong to make such an assumption. The truth is much more complicated than you think. I am going to prove to you tonight that each one of us is born with the memories of our ancestors locked up in our minds. Tonight, through the power of hypnotism, I am going to unlock those memories. And to help me, I would like to ask for a volunteer from the audience.'

Hands were raised throughout the auditorium.

'The young lady in the third row,' Madame Sikursky announced.

A woman stood up and made her way up onto the stage.

'And what is your name?' asked Madame

Sikursky, towering above the volunteer.

'Lucy,' the young woman replied. She sounded nervous.

'Tell me, Lucy,' Madame Sikursky continued, 'have you and I ever met before?'

'No,' Lucy replied.

'And do you speak any foreign languages?'

Lucy shook her head.

'Good. I want you to forget all about the audience. Just close your eyes and concentrate on my voice. Begin by breathing in deeply. Breathe in and out again. In and out, in and out. You are beginning to relax, Lucy. Your arms are hanging limply at your sides. You feel as if your whole body is gradually melting away.'

It seemed to Otto that Madame Sikursky was talking directly to him, not to the young woman on the stage, and he felt *his* body relaxing as she spoke. He felt a great temptation to close his eyes and drift away. But he forced them to stay open so he could see everything that was going on.

'I am going to help you reach far back into your history,' Madame Sikursky told Lucy, 'much further than you have ever been before, back to a time before you were even born. In order for that to be possible, you have to believe in my powers completely. Do you believe?'

'Yes, I believe,' Lucy replied.

Otto found himself repeating the same words in a whisper.

'Your mind is like a tunnel of light,' Madame Sikursky went on. 'And you are travelling along that tunnel, slowly at first, but getting faster all the time.'

Otto found himself envying the woman on the stage. He wanted to be travelling along that tunnel of light.

'As you travel through the tunnel the years slip past you,' Madame Sikursky continued. 'One year, two years, ten years, fifty years, a hundred years, two hundred and fifty years. And stop! You have travelled back to a time before you were even born, to the life of one of your ancestors. You are no longer in a tunnel, Lucy. You are in the past. Look around you and tell me what you see.'

'I see a young girl standing in a field,' Lucy announced.

The audience gasped and Otto gasped with them. This was no fraud, he was certain of it.

'Do you know this girl?' Madame Sikursky asked,

'Yes I do.' Lucy sounded genuinely surprised. 'Her name is Marie-Claire.'

'And where is this field?'

'In Normandy.'

'Do you know what language Marie-Claire speaks?'

'French, of course.'

'Can you speak to Marie-Claire in her own language?'

'Yes, I think so.'

'Then will you please ask Marie-Claire what year it is?'

Lucy said something in French. Then she paused, as if listening, and Otto listened too, straining his ears for a response from Lucy's invisible companion.

After a short pause Lucy announced, 'Marie-Claire tells me that it is 1759.'

'Thank you Lucy,' Madame Sikursky said. She proceeded to suggest several more questions, all of which Lucy relayed to someone she could clearly see but who was invisible to the audience.

After Lucy's invisible ancestor had described

what she had eaten for breakfast, what the weather was like and how she had spent that morning, Madame Sikursky decided that the audience had heard enough. 'Now we are going to say goodbye to Marie-Claire,' she announced. 'So just concentrate on my voice once more. You are back in the tunnel of light, and you are travelling along that tunnel, slowly at first but getting faster all the time. The years slip past you. One year, two years, ten years, fifty years, a hundred years, two hundred and fifty years. And stop! You are back in your own time once more. When I click my fingers you will open your eyes and you will find yourself standing upon the stage of the Belsham Theatre in Bridlington Chawley.'

Madame Sikursky clicked her fingers and Lucy gave a little shudder, then opened her eyes and looked around her in confusion, like a person who has just woken up from a very deep sleep.

The audience clapped and Otto joined in enthusiastically.

Juliet refused to clap, however. 'If you ask me, that young woman was a plant,' she said dismissively. 'She probably gets paid by

Madame Sikursky to go up there and spout all that stuff. What do you think, Otto?'

Otto made no reply. He was scarcely even aware that Juliet was addressing him. His mind was full of Madame Sikursky's voice, so melodious, so attractive, so inviting. He wanted to hear her speaking *his* name. It seemed like the most exciting thing that could possibly happen to him.

'Now I would like to ask another member of the audience to join me up here on the stage,' Madame Sikursky said.

Immediately Otto raised his hand.

'Otto, what are you doing?' Juliet whispered. She grabbed hold of his arm but it was too late. Madame Sikursky was pointing in his direction.

Otto got to his feet.

'Sit down, Otto!' Maximillian ordered – but as far as Otto was concerned his friends could have been in another room. Their words seemed faint and indistinct; they meant nothing whatsoever to him. The voice of Madame Sikursky was all he wished to listen to. She had issued a summons that he could not possibly ignore. Shaking off Juliet's grasp, he made his way to the end of the aisle and walked boldly up towards the stage.

Up close, Madame Sikursky was even more striking than when seen from afar. She was very tall, her skin was almost unnaturally pale and her long hair was jet black apart from a pure white lock at the front. Her eyes seemed huge and the irises so dark, they were almost black.

She asked Otto his name and began to repeat the process she had been through with Lucy. Otto felt his breathing slowing down, his body relaxing and in his mind a tunnel of light appeared – just as she had described it. Travelling along that tunnel was pleasant enough at first. Otto could feel the years passing, one after another, and he could hear a great tapestry of sound – people speaking, babies crying, the hum of car engines, bursts of music, waves crashing. Then, as the speed of his passage through the tunnel began to increase, his awareness of each individual year was lost and the background noises blurred together in a great *whoosh* of sound and he was hurtling backwards through time like a piece of debris flung far out into space by a powerful explosion.

'Stop!' Madame Sikursky's voice cut through everything and the tunnel of light vanished as if she had flipped a switch in his head.

'What can you see around you, Otto?'

He was standing in a circular room. The walls were of stone – but in places elaborate tapestries had been hung showing animals being hunted and battles being fought. At intervals, narrow openings in the wall offered a view of roof after roof stretching as far as the eye could see, and somehow Otto knew that those roofs belonged to the ancient city of Babylon.

Reclining on a couch at the other side of the room was a plump, bearded man. He was dressed in a long white robe and sandals. A purple cloak hung over his shoulders, held in place by an elaborate golden clasp. He was looking in Otto's direction but it was clear that Otto was invisible to him.

Just as the man in the purple cloak could not see Otto, Otto could no longer see Madame Sikursky, or the Belsham Theatre for that matter. Indeed, he had entirely forgotten the theatre's existence. But he could hear Madame Sikursky's voice inside his head.

'What is the name of the man in the

purple cloak?' she asked.

Otto was about to say that he had no idea but then he realised that he knew the man's name perfectly well. 'Balshazzar,' he said, feeling the level of Madame Sikursky's interest rising as he said it. It was as though the air surrounding him had suddenly got warmer. But he knew that it was not really physical warmth he felt, it was Madame Sikursky's excitement.

'What is Balshazzar doing, Otto?' she asked, eagerly.

Balshazzar was thinking. A frown creased his forehead and every now and again he would look down at a flat, oblong clay tablet covered with markings that looked like writing. Otto had a strong conviction that he would be able to understand the writing if he was just given time enough; he was about to report this to Madame Sikursky when an urgent clamouring noise began to fill his head. He had no idea what was producing this noise, only that it was impossible to ignore.

Louder and louder the noise grew and at the same time the room in the tower began to tremble as if it were merely painted upon a piece of silk that was rippling gently in the breeze. A moment later the tower and its bearded inhabitant was gone. Otto was standing on the stage of the Belsham Theatre once more.

A man in a bow tie and tuxedo was speaking into a microphone. '… so I must ask you all to vacate the building in an orderly fashion,' he was saying. 'And please remember, there is absolutely no need to panic.'

Madame Sikursky was glaring at the man as if she would have liked to hit him. 'This is ridiculous!' she declared angrily. 'I've never had anything like this happen before and I can tell you I've performed in almost every major city in the world.'

'I'm very sorry, madam,' the man replied, 'but we can discuss all this later. For now I must ask you to vacate the theatre along with everyone else.' He turned to Otto. 'And you too, please,' he added.

'I don't understand,' Otto said. He was still in a daze from his hypnotic experience and his mind was unable to grasp what was happening.

'It's a fire alarm,' the man explained. 'That means everyone needs to leave the theatre right away. Now there's an exit just behind the stage, if you go down the steps and turn left, you'll see it right in front of you.'

But before Otto could move, his arm was seized in a vice-like grip. He turned to see Madame Sikursky towering over him. 'Not before you tell me your full name and address,' she insisted. 'You and I have a great deal of important business together.'

Until now Otto had found Madame Sikursky utterly fascinating, as if she were some wonderful, kind and trusted friend. But suddenly she seemed to have changed. There was a steely determination in her voice and a dangerous glitter in her eye as if she would not tolerate disobedience of any kind.

'Your full name and address,' she repeated.

Otto opened his mouth to reply but before he could do so Juliet and Maximillian appeared on the stage beside him.

'No time for that now, Otto,' Maximillian said. 'We have to leave the theatre immediately.'

He quickly steered Otto behind the stage curtain, down a flight of steps and out into the street. 'My car's parked round the corner,' he said. 'I'll give you both a lift home.'

'What about the fire?' Otto asked as they

made their way towards the theatre's car-park.

'There wasn't a fire,' Maximillian told him. 'I set the fire alarm off, that's all.'

'Why?'

'Because you were standing up on the stage telling everybody and his uncle that you are descended from one of the most powerful magicians ever to have walked the earth, that's why,' Maximillian replied. 'Whatever possessed you to go up onto the stage in the first place?'

'I don't know,' Otto said. He tried to remember what he had been thinking when he got up from his seat and headed towards the stage. 'It was her voice,' he said finally. 'I couldn't help myself.'

'Hmm! That sounds more like magic than hypnotism,' Maximillian observed.

'Do you know those men, Max?' Juliet interrupted. She had been quietly walking along on the other side of Otto, pondering what had happened, but now she was staring straight ahead with a look of alarm on her face.

Maximillian took no notice of her question. 'You know I've got a feeling that this is why Madame Sikursky was performing in

Bridlington Chawley in the first place,' he continued. 'I should have thought of something like this. What a fool I am!'

'Max, I said, do you know those men?' Juliet repeated, speaking more urgently this time.

'I suppose she could have set up some sort of magical search that directed her to Bridlington Chawley,' Maximillian continued, still completely oblivious to Juliet's question, 'but why? That's what I'd like to know.'

'Max!' Juliet repeated, grabbing him by the arm and shaking him. 'I said, do you know those men?'

'What men?' Maximillian replied. He sounded more than a little irritated at being interrupted in the middle of a train of thought.

'Those three men standing next to your car,' Juliet said.

Maximillian stopped in his tracks. In front of his gleaming red sports car stood three muscle-bound men with shaven heads, their arms folded across their chests. 'I think perhaps we'd better…' he began.

But it was too late. Two of the men put their hands in their breast pockets and pulled out guns.

Otto stood rooted to the spot, too frightened to even blink.

The third man was dressed in a suit and tie, unlike the other two who wore jeans and casual jackets. Somehow this made him look even more menacing. Now he stepped forwards and treated them to an icy smile.

'Maximillian Hawksmoor, I believe,' he said. 'And this would be Otto Spinoza and Juliet Pennington, unless I'm very much mistaken. You're earlier than we expected.'

'Who are you?' Maximillian demanded.

'You'll find out soon enough,' the smartly-dressed thug replied. He pointed with his thumb towards an anonymous white van that was parked beside Maximillian car. 'In the back of the van, all three of you!' he ordered.

'What if we say no?' Otto said. He tried to sound brave and defiant but he could hear his own voice shaking.

'Much better if you didn't,' the man replied, shaking his head. 'We don't want any bloodshed, now do we?'

'I think we'd better do as he says,' Maximillian suggested.

'That's more like it,' the man agreed.

He opened the rear doors of the van and they climbed inside. There were no seats so they had to sit on the floor with their backs against the side of the van. The two armed men climbed in after them and sat directly opposite, their guns still held out in front of them.

'And please don't try any of your magic tricks Mr Hawksmoor,' the smartly-dressed thug said. 'My men are trained to shoot the instant anything unexpected happens.'

Maximillian nodded. 'I understand,' he said.

Otto put his arms around his knees and hugged them to his chest. A voice in his head kept telling him there was a strong chance he might not come out of this alive. He glanced at Juliet and saw she was as white as a sheet and there was terror written across her face. Then his eyes met Maximillian's. A pale smile flitted across Max's face. 'Hang on in there, Otto,' it seemed to say. Otto nodded and took a deep breath. Then the doors of the van were slammed shut, the engine started up and they were in motion.

2

THE MAN WHO DIDN'T EXIST

There were no windows in the van so it was impossible to see where they were going, and Otto, Juliet and Maximillian's captors refused to answer any of their questions. 'You'll find out soon enough,' was the only comment they were prepared to make.

The journey took about an hour and a half – long enough for them to have reached the outskirts of London if they had been travelling north, Otto worked out, or the coast if their direction was southwards.

It was not very comfortable in the van. There were no cushions, no seat belts, just the cold metal floor that transmitted every bump in the road into Otto's spine. By the time they finally came to a halt, he felt stiff and sore from sitting in one position for so long.

The rear doors opened and the smartly-dressed thug reappeared. 'Out you come. Nice and slowly. No tricks,' he said.

Otto and the others clambered gratefully out, only to find themselves deep in the bowels of an underground car park. 'Follow me,' the smartly-dressed thug.

Otto hesitated briefly, gazing round to see if there was anything that might offer a clue to their whereabouts, but then one of the other thugs nudged him in the ribs with his gun. He quickly did as he was told.

They stepped into a lift and the smartly-dressed thug selected the twelfth floor. There was a brief sensation of movement and a sinking feeling in Otto's stomach, then the lift stopped. The doors slid open and they stepped out into an anonymous grey-carpeted, white-walled corridor. The smartly-dressed thug led the way, stopping in front of a door on which the letters DOI had been neatly stencilled. He knocked once, then opened the door and shepherded Otto, Juliet and Maximillian inside. The other thugs stayed outside in the corridor.

Otto found himself standing in a large modern office. The blinds were drawn, preventing any view to the outside world. Behind the desk, frowning at a computer screen sat an immensely fat man with a shiny bald head. He looked up and nodded at the smartly-dressed thug.

'Well done, Number Seven,' he said. 'I knew I could rely on you.' Then he clasped his hands together and rocked back on his chair with a look of great satisfaction on his face. 'Mr Hawksmoor, Master Spinoza, Miss Pennington, I must say I've been looking forward to this meeting *ever* so much.'

'Who are you?' Maximillian asked.

'You can call me Mr Jones if you like,' the fat man replied. 'It's not my real name of course. But then it's such a long time since I've used my real name that I forget it myself sometimes.'

'Why have you brought us here?' Otto demanded.

'Because I need your help,' Mr Jones replied.

'We don't help people who threaten us with guns,' Juliet said.

'Is that so? Well perhaps you might change your mind when you see what I've got in the next room. Pull back the curtain, Number Seven.'

The rear wall of the office was covered by a thick black curtain which Number Seven now drew back. He revealed a glass partition that allowed them to see directly into the adjoining smaller room. In the centre was a large black cat with a glossy coat and a remarkably thick tail. A chain was attached to a collar round his neck and secured to a metal ring in the floor. It is not always easy to tell what a cat is thinking but in this case there was no doubt. He looked thoroughly dejected.

'Corny!' Juliet said, miserably.

'Exactly,' Mr Jones replied. 'Your little furry friend. You wouldn't believe the trouble he gave us getting him here. Scratched my men terribly.'

'Good!' Juliet said.

'You can't keep him locked up like that,' Otto said. 'It's cruel.'

'Oh but we can,' Mr Jones replied. 'We can do anything we like. You know there are plenty of people in my organisation who would be very interested in hearing about a talking cat. I've no doubt they'd want to carry out all sorts of experiments on him.'

'No!' Juliet cried.

'But then they don't have to know about him if you agree to help me with my problem,' Mr

31

Jones went on. 'It can be our little secret. And you needn't worry about him. He's been perfectly well treated. A great deal better than he deserves, if you ask me.'

'Look, I think you'd better tell us what all this is about,' Maximillian said. 'Who are you working for and what exactly do you want us to do?'

'That's much more like it!' Mr Jones said. 'Let's start with who I work for. I'm surprised you haven't guessed already. I work for the government.'

'The government doesn't kidnap people,' Otto pointed out.

'Officially you're quite right,' Mr Jones said. 'Her Majesty's Government would have nothing whatsoever to do with kidnapping. It's not legal. It's not British. But then, *officially*, I don't exist, you see. There is no Mr Jones. If someone were to stand up in the House Of Commons and ask the Prime Minister about me he would simply shake his head and tell you that he has never heard of me.'

'So what is this organisation, then?' Maximillian asked.

'We call ourselves The Department of

Impossibility,' Mr Jones replied. 'Anything that takes place that the rest of the security services can't understand, anything that seems to be contrary to the normal laws of physics, we get to deal with it, whether it's UFOs or elementals – oh yes, we know all about them,' he added when he saw the look of surprise on his captives' faces. 'We've been aware of magical goings-on for some time now. As a matter of fact we've got very substantial files on all three of you. Although I must admit we had no idea about the talking cat until we made his acquaintance.'

'If you know so much about us, why didn't you just politely ask for our help?' Otto demanded.

'Because we couldn't afford to run the risk of telling you all about our little problem, then you saying sorry, we don't want to get involved and walking away with all that top-secret knowledge.'

'We wouldn't have told anyone,' Juliet said. 'You didn't have to kidnap Corny to keep us quiet.'

'So you say, Miss Pennington, but everyone can be made to talk. It's just a matter of finding their weak spot. No, in this department we don't take any chances.'

'What about my mother?' Otto demanded. 'Do you think she won't get suspicious when we don't come back on time?'

Mr Jones smiled. 'It's all been taken care of. Your mother's had a telephone call to inform her that you and Miss Pennington have been asked to take part in a TV recording of the show, so naturally you'll be back considerably later than she expected.

'Now then, let me tell you why I need your assistance. Three months ago a captain in the British Army who was organising a routine mine-clearing operation in Babil Province in Iraq came across a clay tablet. It was covered with writing in some language he did not recognise. A less intelligent soldier might have just have tossed it to one side and forgotten all about it. But not this man. He thought it looked old and possibly valuable, so he showed it to his commanding officer who showed it to a friend of his who just happened to be a world-famous archaeologist. As soon as he saw it the archaeologist got tremendously excited. He recognised that the clay tablet he held in his hand was at least two thousand years old, possibly a great deal more. But of course it was the property of the Iraqi government. Nevertheless, in recognition of the part played by the British Army in discovering this unique piece of history, Iraq agreed to lend it to the British Museum for a period of six months. The museum decided to create a special exhibition featuring the clay tablet as its centre-piece. That exhibition is due to open in four days' time. However, two nights ago the tablet was stolen.'

Maximillian shook his head and tutted. 'How very careless!'

'And now I suppose you want us to get it back for you?' Otto said.

'Precisely, Otto. But first I want you to look at a piece of CCTV footage that shows the actual theft.'

He turned the computer monitor on his desk round to face them and they saw a grainy black and white image of a large empty room in the centre of which was a display case.

'This is the room in the British Museum where the tablet was going to be exhibited,' Mr Jones told them. 'You can see it's already in place in the display case. The clock at the bottom of the screen shows it's just after midnight. Now watch what happens next.'

Quite suddenly there was a figure standing beside the display case. He seemed to have just appeared from nowhere. The man – if it was a man (it wasn't possible to be definite since he was wearing a hood, a face-mask and gloves) took a hammer from a bag on his back, smashed open the display case, picked up the clay tablet and promptly disappeared again.

'You can see why they gave this to my department,' Mr Jones said. 'A thief who materialises in a locked museum in the middle of the night and then de-materializes. Not exactly a run of the mill robbery. But the funny things is, this is not the first time we've come across Mr Now-You-See-Me-Now-You-Don't.'

'He's committed other crimes?' Maximillian asked.

'Oh yes, but they're very different from this one.' Mr Jones picked up a sheet of paper that was lying on his desk. 'In the last six months he's been responsible for nineteen robberies, twelve of which have taken place in pharmacies where he has stolen boxes of headache tablets, six in supermarkets where he has stolen boxes

36

of breakfast cereal and bottles of milk and one in a sports shop where he stole a complete set of golf clubs and three dozen golf balls.'

'Headache tablets, breakfast cereal and golf clubs?' Otto repeated. 'That's downright weird!'

'You're telling me,' Mr Jones continued. 'In each case we have CCTV footage of him appearing and disappearing in the middle of the night. There are no fingerprints, no forensic evidence, and no clues. Now, obviously we can't have the public hearing about this sort of thing. They might start to panic. So we've been forced to bribe the shop owners to keep quiet about it. That was all right when he was just stealing cornflakes and paracetamol, but a priceless exhibit from the British Museum is an altogether different business. He has to be caught. And quickly. The Iraqi government don't yet know that we've lost their precious clay tablet. If we have to tell them, it could provoke a serious diplomatic incident.'

'And you might lose your job,' Juliet suggested.

Mr Jones' eyes narrowed. 'How very astute you are, young lady. Yes, as you correctly point out, I might lose my job. But if that were to be the case, then I can assure you that you would also lose your little furry friend in the next room. Do I make myself clear?'

Juliet said nothing but if looks could kill, Mr Jones would have been dead and buried.

'We get the point,' Maximillian told him.

'Good, then I take it you agree to help me?'

'On one condition,' Maximillian said. 'We need to know that it really is Corny next door and that he hasn't been mistreated. So first of all we go next door *by ourselves* and talk to him. Is it a deal?'

Mr Jones frowned. 'And let you carry out one of your magic tricks? I don't think so, Mr Hawksmoor.'

Maximillian shook his head. 'Tricks are for fools,' he said. 'Not for a man like you, Mr Jones. You didn't get to be in charge of the most secret department of the government's secret service by being a fool. You're a very clever man. I understand that.'

As Maximillian spoke it seemed to Otto that his hands which rested apparently harmlessly in his lap, fluttered ever so slightly, the fingers twitching faintly as if an electric current had run through them.

'Your agents are highly trained,' Maximillian went on. He turned towards the smartly-dressed thug. 'Number Seven can wait outside in the corridor. He wouldn't let us get away with anything. He delivered us here, didn't he? He knows what he's doing.'

Again the faintest suggestion of movement rippled through Maximillian's fingers.

'Besides, you can watch everything that happens through the glass. All we want is to speak to Corny by ourselves without anyone else being present in the room to put pressure on him. That way we can establish exactly what's happened and if he really hasn't been harmed, like you say, you've got yourself a deal.'

Mr Jones hesitated then shrugged. 'As you wish,' he said. 'But remember, Number Seven will be outside the door the whole time and I will be watching through the glass.'

Maximillian put out his hand. 'Let's shake on the bargain Mr Jones.'

Mr Jones looked at Maximillian's extended hand for a moment with a slightly confused expression. Then he reached across the desk and took it.

The hand shake seemed to go on for a very long time as the two men looked deep into each other's eyes. It was Maximillian who let go first. 'You're a smart man, Mr Jones,' he said, 'a real professional.'

Mr Jones smiled and nodded to Number Seven who opened the door and followed Maximillian, Otto and Juliet out into the corridor. The other thugs were still waiting outside, one at either end of the corridor. The men watched with narrowed eyes as Number Seven led the captors to the door of the adjoining room. 'I'll be waiting right here,' he reminded them.

Once inside, they closed the door behind them. Cornelius looked a picture of self-pity. 'You took your time,' he said unhappily.

'Poor Corny!' Juliet exclaimed crouching down beside him and stroking his back.

'You've no idea how badly I've been treated,' Cornelius went on. 'You should have seen the food they offered me. If you ask me it was dog food. I told them they could eat it themselves.'

'Corny, be quiet and listen to me!' Maximillian said, kneeling down beside him and beginning to undo the collar and chain.

'We're going to get you out of here but you need to do exactly as I say.'

'Wait a minute, Max, Mr Jones can see you undoing the chain – he can see everything we do in here,' Otto reminded him.

Maximillian shook his head. I took the opportunity to enchant him when we were shaking hands,' he said. 'Just a very simple wish-fulfilment spell.'

'What does that mean?' Juliet asked.

'It means that when he looks through the glass partition he will see exactly what he wants to see. That and a bit of magical flattery should keep him feeling that everything is under control for a little while. But we haven't got time to waste. Now then, Corny, I'm going to have to pluck out one of your whiskers.'

'Pluck out one of my whiskers!' Corny repeated incredulously.

'I'm sorry but it has to be done,' Maximillian assured him. 'I need it to create a simulacrum.'

'What's a simulacrum?' Otto asked.

'It's a copy,' Maximillian told him. 'It will look exactly like Corny but it won't be real. It won't talk or eat and although it will be solid enough to begin with, in a few hours it will begin to fade. But it should give us enough time to get out of here with the real Corny.' He turned back to Corny. 'I'm sorry about this,' he said. 'Please try not to make a noise.' With that he reached forward and swiftly pulled out one of Cornelius' whiskers. To his credit the cat made only a low growl.

Maximillian placed the whisker on the ground, closed his eyes and began muttering quietly. At the same time his hands began passing backwards and forwards over the whiskers in a series of complicated movements. After a few moments, the atmosphere in the room began to thicken as the magic took hold. Maximillian's fingers left trails of coloured light as they moved. A smoky mass began to gather around the whisker, taking on form and substance with every passing second until there were now two cats standing side by side. The real Corny backed away and hissed at his double. A fraction of a second later the simulacrum did exactly the same thing.

'For goodness sake, pull yourself together, Corny,' Maximillian ordered. 'I need to get the collar and chain on the simulacrum. If you remain still, so will he.'

'How can I pull myself together when I don't know whether I'm me or him?' Corny grumbled, but he did as he was told nonetheless.

Maximillian fastened the collar and chain on the simulacrum. Then he stood up, closed his eyes, put his two hands out in front of him, crossing them over at the wrists. Then with one quick movement he flung them out on either side of his body. 'Right,' he said, opening his eyes once more. 'That's broken the connection between the two of you. The next thing we have to do is get out of here before this whole illusion starts to disintegrate.'

3

THE FORBIDDEN SPELL

'How are we going to get the real Corny out of here without anyone realising?' Juliet asked.

'We're going to have to disguise him,' Maximillian replied.

Otto looked sceptical. 'How do you disguise a cat?' he said. 'You can't exactly give him a false beard and moustache.'

'It's not going to be easy,' Maximillian conceded. 'I'll have to try a bit of shape-changing.'

'Wait a minute! If you think you're going to mess about with my appearance...' Cornelius began.

'Quiet, Corny!' Maximillian interrupted sharply. 'I'm trying to think. He stood there frowning deeply for a moment, then nodded his head. 'I've got it. Look at me, Corny.'

Cornelius stared unblinking as Maximillian's

hands moved rapidly in a series of gestures that looked a bit like someone sewing with an invisible needle. At the same time he chanted softly in the magical language which Otto and Juliet had heard so many times over the last few months. The temperature in the room rose rapidly and Otto felt his skin begin to prickle. For some reason the presence of magic always made him itchy. Then the electric light flickered off and on again, there was a smell of singed hair and quite suddenly Cornelius had disappeared. In his place was a small black object not much bigger than a coin.

'What have you done to him?' Juliet asked, in alarm.

'Nothing serious, I promise you,' Maximillian said. He bent down, picked up the object that had once been Corny and handed it over. It was a brooch made of shiny black metal fashioned in the shape of a green-eyed cat.

'Is this really him?' Juliet asked in disbelief.

Maximillian nodded. 'Pin it on your blouse and let's get out of here.'

Number Seven was waiting outside in the corridor. When they opened the door he glanced suspiciously into the room. But the sight of the simulacrum satisfied him and he escorted them back to Mr Jones' office with no complaints.

Mr Jones still looked pleased with himself. Clearly, the magical flattery had done its work. 'As you have seen, your pet is quite unharmed,' he told them. 'So now let's get down to business.' He handed over a couple of sheets of printed paper. 'Here is a list of all the shops and supermarkets where the thief has struck and here's a list of people who knew about the tablet. Apart from the soldier who unearthed it in the first place and his commanding officer, they're a mixture of archaeologists and diplomats. We've already investigated them all and we can account for their movements on the night of the robbery. So we're relying on your special abilities to turn up something new. That's it, I'm afraid. We have no other leads. Now my men will drive you home. And remember, if you want your pet back, I need quick results.'

The return to Bridlington Chawley was a great deal more comfortable than the outward journey. They travelled in the back of a sleek black limousine and now that they had agreed to help in the hunt for the stolen tablet, they were allowed to see where they were going. Mr Jones' office was in a perfectly ordinary tower block on the fringes of London. Nobody would have given it a second glance.

But despite the relative comfort in which they travelled, none of them could relax. They had no idea how long it might be before Mr Jones discovered that what he thought was a valuable hostage was really no more than a magical photocopy. Otto kept expecting a mobile phone to ring and the car to turn round and head straight back to Mr Jones' headquarters.

Thankfully, they arrived back at the Belsham Theatre's car park without incident. 'We'll be keeping our eye on you,' Number Seven told them before he drove off with a screech of tyres.

'Not if we can help it,' Otto said when the limousine was out of sight.

'Come on,' Maximillian said. 'Your mother will start worrying if we don't get back soon.'

They got into Maximillian's car and went straight back to the flat above the second-hand bookshop where Otto and his mother lived.

Otto's mother looked relieved to see them.

'I told the man who phoned that they weren't to keep you there all night,' she said. 'Still it must have been exciting being part of a TV recording?' She looked at them all in turn. 'Well aren't you going to tell me about it?'

It was Otto who spoke first. 'Actually, we weren't taking part in a TV recording,' he said.

She frowned and her face took on a look of deep anxiety. 'Has this got something to do with magic?' she demanded. Otto's mother had first hand experience of the magical world. She had been kidnapped by magical creatures called elementals, and Otto, Juliet, Maximillian and Cornelius had been forced to travel to the elemental world to rescue her. Afterwards, she had agreed to allow Otto to join Maximillian's magical detective agency but she was still far from happy about the whole thing.

'I'm afraid so,' Otto admitted. He told her what had really happened and she listened with mounting concern. When he got to the bit where Mr Jones' men had pointed guns at them she turned completely white.

'What are you proposing to do now?' she asked when he finally reached the end of his tale.

'The first thing we're going to do is turn Corny back into a real cat,' Juliet said. She looked expectantly at Maximillian.

'Ah yes,' Maximillian said. 'Unfortunately, that may not be quite as easy as you think.'

'What do you mean?' Juliet demanded indignantly. 'You turned him into a brooch. Now turn him back into a cat.'

'I'm sorry, Juliet,' Maximillian told her. 'I don't think I can. I was under a lot of pressure in that room and I couldn't remember how to make the spell reversible. So I just did the best I could.'

'What?' Juliet looked as though she didn't know whether to hit him or burst into tears.

'Calm down!' he said. 'It's not permanent. The spell will wear off sooner or later.'

'How long will it last?' Juliet demanded.

'I honestly don't know. It could be a few hours, it could be a few weeks.'

'A few weeks!'

'He'll be perfectly all right.' Maximillian assured her. 'There's a sort of in-between place where people go when they're temporarily displaced from their bodies. I've never been there myself but I've read about it in magic books. They all agree that it's like a beautiful garden. Corny's probably sleeping in the sun right now.'

Juliet looked unimpressed. 'People who can't do magic properly shouldn't go around casting spells,' she said, grumpily.

Otto decided it was time to change the subject. 'In the meantime what are we going to do about Mr Jones?' he asked. 'He's expecting us to find his vanishing thief for him, remember.'

'And that's exactly what we're going to do,' Maximillian said.

'I don't see why you should do his job for him,' Mrs Spinoza objected, 'especially now that you've got Corny back. Well, almost,' she added as Juliet opened her mouth to protest.

'Have you ever heard of the Tower Of Babel?' Maximillian asked.

Otto and Juliet shook their heads but Otto's mother nodded. 'It's in the Bible,' she said.

Maximillian nodded. 'The Tower of Babel was built in what is now called Babil province in Iraq.'

'Where Mr Jones' clay tablet came from?' Juliet said.

'Exactly. And where Otto's ancestor, Balshazzar, was king. What most people don't realise is that it was an ancient magical laboratory. All the most powerful magicians of the day were gathered there and their minds were focused on one project – the discovery of the Forbidden Spell.'

'What's that?' Otto asked.

'Far back in the history of the world, a thousand years before even Balshazzar, there was a magician called Shamash. Many people believe he was the most powerful magician who has ever lived. He used magic in a special way, weaving collections of spells together to make bigger and more powerful spells and then weaving those more powerful spells together to make still more powerful ones. One day he realised that he had created a spell so powerful it could destroy the whole world.'

'I don't like the sound of this,' Mrs Spinoza said.

'Neither did Shamash. He was so frightened by what he had made that he gave up magic altogether, destroyed his records and forbade any of his pupils to reveal the nature of the spell. But it's said that knowledge of the

Forbidden Spell was written down secretly and hidden for centuries until Balshazzar's magicians set out to rediscover it. Fortunately for the rest of the world, they blew up the tower in the process and they were all killed.'

'And you think that Mr Jones' clay tablet might have come from that tower?' Otto asked

'I think it's highly likely. It's from the right area. And why else would a magical thief want to steal it from the museum? Consider what this could mean. In the wrong hands the Forbidden Spell could be more destructive than a nuclear bomb.'

'Then we have to get it back as quickly as possible,' Otto said.

'Exactly. But the question is, where to start?'

'Mr Jones gave us a list of all the people who knew about the tablet,' Juliet suggested. 'Why don't we look them up on the computer and see what we can find out about them?'

'Good idea,' Maximillian said.

Otto's mother looked much less impressed. 'It's half past ten,' she said. 'You should really be thinking about going to bed.' But she could see that she was wasting her time. Sleep was the last thing on anyone's mind. She sighed.

'Very well,' she said, 'but try not to stay up all night.'

Otto and Juliet made their way to the small office from which Mrs Spinoza conducted the business of the book shop. They switched on the computer and were soon working their way through the list of names that Mr Jones had given them.

It was pretty dull work. Most of the links suggested by the search engine were scholarly articles about archaeology, as dry as dust and full of long words that they couldn't understand. Otto was beginning to think that this whole approach was a waste of time when they came upon a picture that changed his mind completely.

They had been looking for information about a man called Benjamin Runsiman, a diplomat who had been involved in negotiations between the British Museum and the Iraqi government when Juliet discovered a photograph of him attending a reception at the Iraqi embassy. Dressed in a tuxedo and bow tie, with short, dark hair going grey at the temples, he looked very distinguished. But it wasn't his looks that made them both gasp. It was the woman on his arm. Her face was turned away from the camera so you could only see her profile but there was no mistaking her. It was Madame Sikursky.

Standing behind them, peering over their shoulders at the screen, Maximillian gave a low whistle.

'Quite a coincidence, eh?' Juliet said.

Maximillian shook his head. 'It's more than just a coincidence. First an internationally-famous hypnotist puts on a show in Bridlington Chawley. Then Otto gets up on the stage and lets her regress him to Ancient Babylon. On the way home from the show we're kidnapped by a government agency looking for a stolen clay tablet that just happens to come from Ancient Babylon. Finally we discover that the same internationally-famous hypnotist has been photographed going around with one of the people responsible for bringing the tablet to this country in the first place.'

'So what are you saying?' Juliet asked.

'I'm saying that this looks very like a magically induced improbability cluster.'

Juliet frowned. 'What's that in plain English?' she asked.

'A long time ago magicians noticed that even quite small magic spells sometimes cause clusters of coincidences to happen around them,' Maximillian told her. 'No one knows why exactly, but there are two main theories. One is that magic distorts the normal rules of cause and effect.'

'What are they?' Otto asked.

'The laws of cause and effect? Well, it's quite simple. You drop a glass and it breaks. Letting go of the glass is the cause, the broken glass is the effect. But say a magician drops a glass and then quickly casts a spell to stop it breaking. A cause has taken place without an effect. That's a distortion of the rules. But it doesn't always stop there. Sometimes that distortion creates other distortions, like ripples in a pond. After a while all these little distortions start having a major effect on the everyday world, producing clusters of improbable events. Weird coincidences.'

'OK, but you said there were two theories,' Otto pointed out. 'What's the other one?'

'Oh it's silly, really,' Maximillian Hawksmoor replied. 'In the olden days magicians used to believe that there were these three goddesses called the Fates, who held the threads of all our lives in their hands as they wove the pattern of life. If there was a series of strange coincidences, these old fashioned magicians said it was caused by the Fates, suddenly deciding to change the pattern. But we modern magicians don't believe in stuff like that.'

'So you think we're in the middle of one of these Improbability Clusters right now?' Juliet said.

'Yes I do,' Maximillian told her.

'Is that dangerous?' Otto asked.

'Well it's all right if it stops here,' Maximillian said. 'If there were another coincidence then I would start to get worried.'

He had barely finished speaking when the doorbell rang.

Otto and Juliet glanced at each other. 'You don't think it's Mr Jones and his thugs, do you?' Otto said.

'It might be best if I answered the door,' Maximillian told them.

Otto's mother was already standing on the landing looking anxiously down the stairs. Otto and Juliet joined her.

Maximillian slowly descended the staircase,

ransacking his brain for a spell that might be of some use against a gun but his mind was blank. The blinds were drawn downstairs and the bookshop was in darkness. He blundered about looking for the light switch, muttering distinctly unmagical curses when he banged his shin against one of the bookcases. Finally he found the switch and turned on the lights. The silhouette of a tall, imposing figure was outlined behind the door.

'Might as well get it over with,' Maximillian said to himself.

He crossed the room and opened the door.

Madame Sikursky was standing on the doorstep.

4

THE FACE IN THE MIRROR

'I'm looking for Otto Spinoza,' Madame Sikursky announced. 'I've checked in the phone book and the only Spinoza listed in Bridlington Chawley lives at this address. Have I come to the right place?'

Maximillian Hawksmoor opened and shut his mouth like a fish. He had not expected this and he had no ready answer. Finally he managed to mumble, 'It's very late.'

'Yes,' Madame Sikursky agreed. 'I apologise for troubling you at this time of night but I am most keen to speak to Otto. He does live here, doesn't he?'

'Yes he does,' Otto said. He had crept downstairs to see what was happening and since it was obvious that Maximillian was floundering he had decided to take matters into his own hands. 'I'm Otto Spinoza. What do you want to say to me?'

Madame Sikursky's face lit up. 'Perhaps we could talk about this inside?' she suggested.

Otto hesitated. He remembered how Madame Sikursky's voice had seemed like the most fascinating thing he had ever heard, how he had walked up onto the stage without really realising what he was doing. He strongly suspected her of using magic to enchant him and was just about to say no they could not talk about it inside when a brilliant idea popped into his head. He smiled. 'Certainly,' he said. 'Let's go upstairs.'

Maximillian gave a despairing look as Madame Sikursky stepped into the bookshop, but Otto ignored him and led the beaming hypnotist up the stairs.

'This is my mother,' he said when they reached the landing, 'and this is my friend, Juliet. Mum, this is Madame Sikursky, the world-famous hypnotist. She wants to talk to me.'

'It's a bit late to be making social calls isn't it?' Mrs Spinoza remarked.

'I will not take up very much of your time,' Madame Sikursky said. 'I just had to speak to your son. He is a very special young man.' As she said this, her eyes seemed to glitter greedily.

Otto led Madame Sikursky into the sitting room. 'Let me take your coat,' he said. 'Sit down and make yourself comfortable.'

Madame Sikursky took off her coat and handed it to Otto.

'I'll be back in a moment,' he said.

The others were still standing out in the landing. 'What are you doing?' Juliet hissed.

Otto put his finger to his lips and led them into the kitchen. 'Don't you see?' he said, as soon as the kitchen door was closed. 'This could be our chance to find out something,' he said.

'Such as what?' Juliet demanded.

'Look, she was photographed in the company of one of the diplomats involved in bringing the tablet to England. That's suspicious. Max thinks we need to find the thief so we have to start somewhere.'

'I think it's a really bad idea,' Maximillian said.

'For once, I believe I agree with Max,' Otto's mother added.

'I've got a plan,' Otto told them.

'Well it had better be good,' Juliet replied.

'It is good. Listen, there's only one hotel in

Bridlington Chawley and it's not very far from here. Someone could be there in five minutes if they ran. So if I keep Madame Sikursky busy, Juliet can go to the hotel, get into her room and snoop around.'

'To look for what, exactly?' Juliet demanded.

'I don't know,' Otto said. 'Use your hunchability.'

Hunchability is the instinctive sense that every magical detective relies on. Maximillian had introduced them to it the previous summer.

'That's all very well, Otto, but think about what happened back in the theatre,' Maximillian objected. 'That woman will open up your head like a can of beans.'

'You said we could be in the middle of a magically induced improbability cluster,' Otto pointed out. 'You said that something very big could be happening. Well how else are we going to learn what it is? We are supposed to be investigators, remember. Besides, I'm pretty sure I can resist her this time.'

Maximillian looked unconvinced.

'Listen Max, something tells me I have to do this,' Otto went on. 'It feels like fate, or something.'

'There's no such thing as fate,' Maximillian insisted. 'I've already explained that.'

'Well I'm sorry to be a party-pooper but I don't like this one little bit,' Mrs Spinoza said.

'Mum, you and Max will be in the room the whole time,' Otto said. 'If you think I'm in any danger you can call a halt to the proceedings.'

'It may be too late by then. That woman hasn't come here because she likes your face, Otto. She wants something from you and she looks to me like the kind of person who usually gets what she wants.'

Otto decided it was time to play the ace up his sleeve. 'Don't you think this is what Dad would have done?' he said. 'He didn't hesitate to investigate when he came across that old map that led him to the fountain, he wasn't afraid to rush into a burning house to save my life. If he'd stopped to think about the danger I wouldn't even be here.'

At the mention of her husband a tear came into Mrs Spinoza's eye.

'I want him to be proud of me, Mum,' Otto continued.

Mrs Spinoza took out a handkerchief and blew her nose. 'Very well, Otto,' she said, 'you win.' She turned to Maximillian. 'But I'm relying on you to keep my boy safe. Is that clear?'

'Crystal clear,' Maximillian told her.

'Right then,' said Otto with a grin. 'Let's put the plan into action.'

'How am I supposed to get into her hotel room, anyway?' Juliet asked.

Otto grinned, put his hand in the pocket of Madame Sikursky's coat and drew out a keyring with two keys attached to it.' These might help,' he said.

Juliet nodded. 'OK,' she said. 'I suppose it's worth a try.'

She took the keys and crept silently downstairs and let herself out of the front door, Otto, his mother and Maximillian made their way back into the sitting room. Madame Sikursky had picked up a photograph that stood in a frame on a bookshelf. It showed Otto when he was about six years old holding a football and grinning at the camera. She was studying it as closely as if it were a crucial piece of evidence in a murder case.

Now, however, she turned and gave them her most polished smile. 'I hope you don't mind me saying this Mrs Spinoza, but Otto doesn't look very much like you. Perhaps he takes after his father?'

Otto's mother took the photograph from her and replaced it on the shelf. 'He looks like himself,' she said, making no attempt to sound friendly.

Madame Sikursky could not have failed to notice the hostility in Mrs Spinoza's voice but she carried on smiling broadly. 'Well, I'm sure you all want to know what I'm doing here at this time of night,' she said. 'So I'll explain myself. In my opinion, Otto is an exceptionally interesting boy. His response to hypnotism was so much more intense than what I normally see. As I always say when I give one of my performances, almost everyone can be taken back to a time before they were born but very few people can travel thousands of years into the past. It only happens when the subject is particularly susceptible to hypnotism and where there is something of major importance in his ancestry. And when I say something of major importance I mean an event so significant that it has altered the course of history. For this reason I would like to offer

Otto a course of hypnotism sessions entirely free.' She looked at Otto's mother and then at Maximillian Hawksmoor. 'Many people would be prepared to pay a great deal of money for my services,' she added.

'I don't think…' Mrs Spinoza began.

But Otto interrupted her. 'I think it sounds like a terrific idea. Why don't we start right now?'

Madame Sikursky nodded enthusiastically. 'Yes indeed. There's no time like the present.'

'Or the past,' Otto added.

Madame Sikursky smiled. 'Very good, Otto. I can see we are going to get on like a house on fire.' She turned back to Mrs Spinoza. 'You are happy to allow this to go ahead?'

'I can't say I'm happy,' Mrs Spinoza replied, 'but if it's what Otto wants then I suppose you'd better get on with it.'

'Look confident,' Juliet told herself as she entered the revolving doors of The Hotel Magnifico. 'It will probably be a night porter on duty by now. He won't have any idea who is staying here and who isn't. Just look as if you belong.'

The tag on the key ring that Otto had found in Madame Sikursky's pocket had borne the number 36. Juliet guessed that meant Madame's Sikursky's room was on the third floor. She stepped into the foyer and looked around for a lift. An elderly man in uniform seated behind the reception desk glanced up from the newspaper he was reading. Juliet's heart skipped a beat but she managed to smile at him. He gave her a nod then went back to his paper.

She located the lift and pushed the button. There was a distant clunk and an illuminated arrow indicated that it was on its way down.

'Come on, come on,' Juliet told the lift.

At last the doors opened and she stepped inside, pressing the appropriate button. The doors closed, the lift jerked slightly, then began its ascent.

She got out at the third floor, quickly found room 36 and knocked on the door. When no one answered she looked up and down the corridor. Satisfied that she was unobserved, she took the key out of her pocket and let herself in.

The room was a dreadful mess. There were

several dresses thrown across the bed, a towel lay half in and half out of the bathroom and the floor was littered with shoes. Juliet shook her head and tutted to herself. Her parents would have given her a lecture if she'd left her room in this condition.

'Never mind gaping at the mess, you're here on a mission,' she reminded herself. She began opening drawers and examining their contents.

Meanwhile Otto was sitting in a comfortable armchair and Madame Sikursky perched opposite him on an upright chair. Maximillian Hawksmoor and Mrs Spinoza sat in opposite corners of the room watching the proceedings anxiously.

'I want you to relax,' Madame Sikursky was telling Otto. 'Just listen to my voice and don't think about anything else.'

When she had stood in the doorway of the bookshop Madame Sikursky had seemed like any other person, a little tall and with rather striking looks, perhaps, but that was all. Now, however, as she set about the task of hypnotism, she seemed to gain in power so that she was once more the intimidating figure who had stood on the stage of the Belsham Theatre.

Her voice became smooth and silky. Listening to her was like slipping into a warm bath at the end of a long, tiring day.

'All your cares are drifting away,' Madame Sikursky continued. 'The room around you grows insubstantial and begins to fade, like a dream you once had a long, long time ago.'

Otto was beginning to feel like someone walking down a steep hill who finds himself going faster and faster until he begins to lose control. He remembered how readily he had assured Maximillian that he could resist Madame Sikursky. But it was not going to be as easy as he had thought.

'I want you to look back into your past, Otto,' Madame Sikursky told him, 'back to the stone tower that you visited earlier this evening.'

As she spoke these words, Otto found himself once more travelling along the tunnel of light that led to the world of his ancestors. A moment later he had arrived in the stone tower where Balshazzar, ruler of Babylon, was pacing back and forth talking to an old man with a long white beard who stood in silence, listening respectfully.

'Tell me what you see around you, Otto,'

Madame Sikursky urged him.

Otto struggled to resist – but it was completely hopeless. He had to do as she commanded. 'I am in the stone tower,' he admitted.

'Well done, Otto.' Her voice almost purring with pleasure. 'Now who else is there?'

'Balshazzar and another man with long white hair. I think he is...'

'Go on!'

'I think he is the Chief Magician.'

'Excellent! Do you know what they are talking about?'

Otto listened carefully. At first their conversation seemed no more than a jumble of unidentifiable sounds but after a while he found that he could understand some of it. More and more of the words began to make sense until at last he knew exactly what they were discussing – the Forbidden Spell.

'Tell me all about it,' Madame Sikursky ordered.

It didn't take Juliet long to go through all the drawers and cupboards in Madame Sikursky's hotel room. But she learned nothing that she didn't already know, except for the fact that Madame Sikursky dyed her hair, used a great deal of make-up and possessed a pair of shoes for every day of the week.

'If this is how much luggage she takes on a trip, I'd hate to see what her wardrobe is like at home,' Juliet said to herself.

But she wasn't here to study footwear. She was looking for information. And so far she had found nothing of any use. She was almost on the point of giving up when she remembered that there was another, smaller key on the ring Otto had taken from Madame Sikursky's pocket. She wondered what it was for. Then she remembered that hotels often provide a safe where guests can leave their valuables. Perhaps the small key was the key to a safe. If so, where would the safe be? She stood in the middle of the room and looked around her. Where would *she* hide a safe in a room like this? Then it came to her in a flash. Behind a picture of course!

There were three pictures hanging on the wall. One was a painting of a vase of flowers. The other two were prints of Bridlington Chawley at the beginning of the century.

She tried the two prints first. Nothing. Then she lifted up the painting of the vase of flowers and there, to her delight, was the small metal door of a safe set into the wall.

Feeling very pleased with herself, she took down the painting and laid it carefully on the bed. Then she tried the key in the lock. It turned with a satisfying click and the door of the safe sprang open. To her disappointment, however, it appeared to be completely empty. But when she put her hand in and felt all round the safe just to make sure, she discovered a scrap of paper at the very back. She took it out and examined it. It looked as if it had been torn out of a notebook. A series of words in some unknown language was written on it.

She had hoped for something more revealing than this – an address book or diary, perhaps. Something that would provide them with a clue that might help solve the mystery. But perhaps Maximillian would be able to make something of it.

She sat down on a chair in front of the dressing table and studied the piece of paper more closely. She had no idea what language it was written in. It could have been Madame Sikursky's own language. Or one of those magical languages that Max sometimes used. She read the words out loud.

Immediately, she felt something change in the room, a thickening in the air, a sense of heightened tension. She knew that feeling and she also knew what caused it – magic. Something was happening to the mirror on the dressing table. Its surface turned cloudy and began swirling as though it were filled with smoke. Fear took hold of Juliet, like icy hands clutching her. What had she done?

She wanted to get up and run from the room but she was rooted to the spot as the cloudy depths of the mirror seethed and boiled. Then suddenly the glass cleared once more. But now, instead of gazing at a reflection of the hotel room, she was looking into the face of a middle-aged man.

In many ways it was an interesting face. Handsome and well-groomed, the man in the mirror reminded Juliet of a TV chat-show host. Except that he looked distinctly irritated, as if he'd been disturbed in the middle of an important meeting.

'Who are you?' he demanded angrily. 'Where is Marushka?'

Juliet stared back at him in dismay.

While Juliet was wondering what to say next, Otto was still watching and listening to Balshazzar and his Chief Magician.

'The key to the Forbidden Spell lies in understanding that it is never spoken,' the Chief Magician was saying. 'It is cast in silence.'

'What do you mean?' Balshazzar demanded. 'How can a spell possibly work if it is never spoken?'

Madame Sikursky's voice interrupted this dialogue. 'Tell me what they are talking about,' she demanded.

But before he could reply, Otto noticed something peculiar happening to the tapestry on the wall nearest him. It showed a group of swordsmen fighting beside a river, but now one of the swordsmen turned his head and Otto saw that he had Maximillian Hawksmoor's face. 'Don't tell her anything, Otto!' the face in the tapestry urged. 'If she learns how to use the Forbidden Spell she'll hold the whole world to ransom.'

'Come on now, Otto. I know you can understand what is being said.' Madame Sikursky said, using the same coaxing tone that you might use to calm a suspicious dog. But below the surface there was more than a hint of steel in her voice.

The figure in the tapestry shook its head and put its finger to its lips.

Meanwhile the conversation continued between Balshazzar and the Chief Magician.

'You must think the spell instead of saying it,' the Chief Magician continued. 'You must make the words vibrate inside your head, like a bell that is struck in an empty room, then concentrate on those vibrations making them grow and grow until they fill the whole world.'

'You are disappointing me, Otto!' Madame Sikursky declared. Now her anger was closer to the surface. 'You must stop resisting. You must tell me everything they are saying.'

'They are talking about the Forbidden Spell,' Otto admitted. The words spilled out of him despite all his efforts to stop them.

The figure in the tapestry put its head in its hands in dismay.

'Very good, Otto. Very good, indeed. What do

they say about this spell? Are they discussing how it should be cast?'

Juliet stared at the man in the mirror in horrified fascination.

'What do you mean by summoning me?' the man in the mirror demanded angrily. 'If this is a trick, you will pay for it, I promise you.'

She should have sprung from the chair and fled the room, but the magic bound her to the spot and the eyes of the man in the mirror bored into hers as if he could see right through to her soul.

'You are no magician,' he said scornfully. 'You are no more than a child. Who has sent you? Who is your master?'

She had to find some way to break the spell. But what did she really know about magic? She had watched Maximillian at work but that was all. She had no powers of her own. She recalled that it was by repeating the words on the piece of paper that she'd got into this predicament. Perhaps if she tried repeating them again... With an enormous effort she tore her gaze away from the man in the mirror and muttered the words of the spell.

It made absolutely no difference.

'If you do not explain yourself immediately, I will turn you to dust,' the man in the mirror threatened.

How do you break a spell? Juliet asked herself. How do you reverse something that you never meant to set in motion?

Reverse! Of course. It had to be worth a try.

For the second time she fought to free her gaze from the man in the mirror. It was even harder this time but somehow she managed it. She looked down at the scrap of paper. She was quite sure that she would have only one chance. So she had to get it right first time. No hesitations, no stumbling over words.

Her brow furrowed with concentration as she read out the words of the spell backwards.

The face in the mirror was a mask of fury. 'How dare you!' he screamed. But it was too late. The mirror was growing cloudy again, the whole room seemed to twist and turn and for a moment Juliet felt as if she might be sick. Then it was over and the mirror showed only a reflection of the room.

Juliet breathed a huge sigh of relief. She stuffed the scrap of paper in her pocket, closed and locked the door of the safe, replaced the picture and glanced around the room. It wasn't exactly as she'd found it but it would have to do. She had to get back to the bookshop before Madame Sikursky picked Otto's brains as clean as a carcass in the desert.

5

A Sacrifice

Madame Sikursky was growing impatient. 'Tell me everything that the old man is saying,' she commanded.

Otto looked desperately at the tapestry on the wall. Every one of the swordsmen turned their heads simultaneously in his direction. They all had Maximillian's face. Each one held his finger to his lips and shook his head frantically.

The trouble was it didn't help. Otto already knew that he shouldn't tell Madame Sikursky what the Chief Magician had just said. He just couldn't help himself. He was no longer in control of what he said or did.

Despairingly he opened his mouth to speak – but in an instant everything changed. The force that had gripped his will, making it do whatever Madame Sikursky demanded, suddenly released him from its clutches.

'What do you mean?' Madame Sikursky said. 'I don't know what you're talking about. A girl? I don't know of any girl.' It was quite clear that she was no longer addressing her comments to Otto. In fact, she seemed to have forgotten all about him.

The scene in the stone tower shimmered and dissolved. Otto blinked and found that he was back in his own living room once more. Madame Sikursky still sat opposite him but she seemed to be staring into space.

'I'll come at once,' she declared, speaking to some unknown and invisible presence. She got to her feet. 'My coat!' she demanded. 'Where is my coat?'

Maximillian left the room and returned a moment later clutching her coat.

'I'm afraid we must continue the session another time,' Madame Sikursky announced as she struggled into her coat. 'Something very important has come up.' With that, she rushed from the room.

'I wonder what's got into her?' Mrs Spinoza said. 'Who was she speaking to?'

'Something to do with Juliet, I expect,' Maximillian replied. 'I think I'd better go after her in case it turns nasty.'

Still dazed, Otto looked from one of them to the other. Then suddenly it dawned on him that Juliet might be in danger, and all because of his suggestion to snoop about in Madame Sikursky's hotel room. 'Wait! I'll come with you,' he said.

They set off for the hotel at a run but they were only a few streets from home when they saw something that made Otto's blood run cold. A white van was cruising slowly down the street – and heading towards them.

Quickly, they ducked into a shop doorway.

A moment later, the van pulled up beside the kerb. From the shadows, Otto and Maximillian watched as Number Seven, in the driving seat of the van, took out a street map and began studying it.

'They're looking for us,' Otto hissed. 'What are we going to do?'

Maximillian bent down and began rummaging in the leather bag that he always carried with him.

'Are you going to cast a spell?' Otto asked.

'Magic is not always the best solution,' Maximillian replied. He straightened up and when he turned round Otto saw that he was now sporting a thick black beard and moustache.

'Wait here!' he ordered. Then he stepped out into the streetlight.

The window of the white van rolled down. 'Excuse me,' said Number Seven. 'I'm looking for Spinoza's Bookshop.'

Maximillian nodded. 'Oh aye,' he said in a broad Scottish accent. 'You're in the wrong part of town, laddie.'

Otto cringed. Maximillian was laying on the accent pretty thickly. But it seemed to convince Number Seven who listened carefully as Maximillian gave a series of directions that would take him out of Bridlington Chawley and halfway up the motorway to London.

'Thanks a lot,' Number Seven said when Maximillian had finished. He turned the van round and drove off in the opposite direction.

'I didn't know you were an actor as well as a magician,' Otto said, stepping out from the shadow of the doorway.

'Some people might say that acting is a kind of magic,' Maximillian replied. 'But it may not keep our friends from the Department of

Impossibility busy for very long. We've got to go and find Juliet before someone else does.'

While Maximillian had been posing as a helpful Scotsman, Juliet was stepping out into the hotel corridor and locking the door behind her. Briefly, she considered what she ought to do with the key. Perhaps it would be best to leave it in the lock. That way Madame Sikursky might think she'd simply forgotten to take it out.

At that moment however, Juliet heard the ping of the lift. There was no time to think! Dropping the key on the carpet, she took to her heels and fled down the corridor. She had only just ducked round the corner when the lift doors opened and Madame Sikursky stepped out.

Juliet quickly found a fire escape which led to some stairs. She took them downwards, two at a time. The night porter looked up in surprise as she rushed through the foyer. He opened his mouth to speak but she didn't give him a chance. For all she knew, Madame Sikursky might be right behind her.

She ran in the direction of the bookshop, wishing her shoes didn't clatter so much on the pavement. Halfway there she bumped into Otto. It took her a few moments to realise that the tall bearded man beside him was Maximillian.

'Are you all right?' Otto asked.

She nodded. 'I'm fine – but only just.'

'Did you find anything helpful?' Maximillian asked.

'Only this.' She handed him the scrap of paper. 'It was in a wall safe. When I spoke it out loud a man appeared in the mirror and threatened to turn me to dust. Fortunately, he disappeared again when I said it backwards.'

Maximillian raised one eyebrow. 'That was smart thinking,' he said. He studied the words on the piece of paper and nodded. 'This is very interesting,' he said, 'very interesting indeed. Let's get back to the bookshop and talk about it there.'

When they got back home Maximillian pulled off his false beard and rubbed his face. 'First things first,' he said. 'Mr Jones' men could come back at any time. We need to disguise the bookshop.'

'You can't disguise a whole bookshop,' Otto protested. 'What are you going to do? Hang your beard on the front door?'

'That won't be necessary,' Maximillian told him. He turned to Otto's mother. 'I'm afraid I'm going to have to ask you to make a sacrifice,' he said.

She looked at him in alarm. 'What sort of sacrifice?'

'That's up to you,' Maximillian told her, 'just something that means a lot to you. It could be a piece of jewellery, an item of clothing, an ornament. It really doesn't matter what it is so long as it's something you've treasured. Can you think of anything like that?'

Mrs Spinoza sat in silence for a while. Then she got up and left the room. A few minutes later she came back with a photograph and handed it over. It was an old black and white snap of a young couple standing on a beach with their arms around each other.

Otto peered over Maximillian's shoulder and gazed at the picture. 'Who is it?' he asked.

His mother smiled. 'Don't you recognise the woman?'

Otto shook his head.

'It's me and your father before we got married,' she told him. 'It's the only photograph I have of him from when we were young.'

Maximillian nodded gravely. 'Thank you, Mrs Spinoza,' he said. 'That will be perfect.' He placed the photograph in a saucer in the centre of the kitchen table, struck a match and set fire to it.

Mrs Spinoza turned her face away as the photograph curled up at the edges and it changed from brown to black, finally crumbling away altogether. All the while Maximillian chanted softly. The words of the spell sounded something like this:

na badari ku sanam
enna kaki bagaram
ki sipani enna kayta
sila mena zunam tay

Otto shuddered slightly, the prickling feeling which always accompanied the presence of magic felt stronger than usual this time and he had the distinct feeling that he could almost understand the words of Maximillian's chant. Almost, but not quite. *I suppose I must be getting more used to magic*, he told himself.

When it was finished Maximillian crumbled the charred photograph to ash, then divided the ash into two piles. Otto followed him downstairs as he bent down and rubbed one

85

pile of ash on the inside door handle. Then he opened the door and rubbed the other half on the outside door handle. Finally, he turned his back on the door, closed his eyes and clapped three times.

'Is that it?' Otto asked. There had been no flash of light, nothing to show that magic had just taken place.

Maximillian smiled. 'A magical camouflage spell disguises itself as well as the object of the spell. But I think you'll find it's worked.'

'I can still see the shop,' Otto pointed out.

'That's because you're in it. Take a walk down to the end of the road and come back.'

Otto did as he was told. Despite Maximillian's assurances, Otto had his doubts about this working. Disguising a whole shop was a tall order. Perhaps it would be more sensible to consider moving out of Bridlington Chawley altogether for the time being, though where they might go he could not imagine.

He got to the end of the road, turned round and headed for home. But when he got to where the shop should have been, it wasn't there. The estate agent's office next door was there and so was the jeweller on the other side.

Otto stared at the point where the two shops met. There was no room for a bookshop.

'Turn round!' It was Maximillian's voice but it wasn't clear where it was coming from.

'What do you mean?' Otto asked.

'Just turn round so that your back is to the shops.'

Otto did as he was told.

'Now look over your left shoulder.'

Otto couldn't believe it! There was Maximillian standing in the doorway of the bookshop, waving to him.

'Just come in backwards,' Maximillian told him.

'That is some spell!' Otto said as he backed into the shop looking over his shoulder the whole time.

Maximillian shook his head. 'The spell was nothing,' he said. 'It's the sacrifice that counts. Your parents must have really been in love, Otto.'

When they were all back in the kitchen, Otto's mother made four mugs of tea and opened a packet of chocolate biscuits while Juliet described in detail everything that had happened in the hotel room.

'You did extremely well,' Maximillian said when she'd finished.

'But I still don't know what it was all about,' Juliet replied.

'The words on the piece of paper are a summoning spell,' Maximillian told her. 'They're a way of speaking to someone from the elemental world.'

'Then the man in the mirror was an elemental?'

Maximillian shook his head. 'That's the odd thing,' he said. 'He's as human as you or I.'

'How do you know that?' Otto asked.

'Because his name is written here in the middle of the spell. Lucas Mendicant. Does that ring a bell with any of you?'

They all shook their heads.

'Lucas Mendicant was a professor of archaeology at Haverstock University,' Maximillian told them, 'and one of the world's leading experts on Ancient Babylon. Haverstock, as you probably know, is a very old university with beautiful old buildings. People come from all over the world to admire the architecture. But the same buildings that look so marvellous in tourists' holiday snaps can be very cold and draughty to work in. So the university began a fundraising programme to modernise the campus, and who do you think they put in charge of it?'

'Lucas Mendicant?' Otto suggested.

'Exactly! And at first it seemed like the perfect choice. He was extremely good at talking people into donating money. He raised over three million pounds in just six months. Then one morning he just disappeared taking all the money with him. And until this evening nobody had found a trace of him.'

'So he's hiding in the elemental world?' Otto said.

'Looks like it,' Maximillian replied.

'Do you think he's the one who stole the clay tablet?' Juliet asked.

'Without a shadow of a doubt.'

'And Madame Sikursky is trying to find out how it works for him,' Otto observed.

'Exactly.'

'Well it looks like we've cracked the case,' Otto said with a grin. 'Now all we have to do is travel to the elemental world and get the tablet back.'

Maximillian shook his head. 'I'm afraid it's

not that simple, Otto. For one thing we don't know where in the elemental world Lucas Mendicant is hiding.'

'You didn't know where I was being held when I was kidnapped by elementals last summer,' Otto's mother pointed out, 'but you still managed to find me.'

'Ah yes, but in that case we had a clue,' Maximillian told her. 'We found green sand on the floor of the bookshop that could only have come from one location. But in this case we have no evidence. We need to look for clues. That's how detectives work, remember?'

'Madame Sikursky must know where he is,' Juliet pointed out.

'Yes, but she's not going to tell us, is she?' Maximillian said.

'Wait a minute! What about Benjamin Runsiman?' Otto suggested, 'You know – the diplomat with whom Madame Sikursky was photographed going to that reception.'

'Of course!' Maximillian said. 'Why didn't I think of that? We must find out where he lives, then go and see what he's got to say about all this.'

Otto's mother frowned. She picked up the

newspaper that was lying on the table and began leafing rapidly through its pages. Then she stopped and nodded. 'I knew that name rang a bell,' she said. She looked up from the newspaper. 'I'm afraid you won't find it easy to interview him.'

'Why not?' Otto asked.

'Because according to this paper he was buried yesterday afternoon. Listen. Doctor Benjamin Runsiman, the British diplomat who was found strangled in his bed at the end of February, was finally laid to rest in Harford cemetery today.'

'Just our luck!' Otto said miserably.

'The end of February,' Maximillian Hawksmoor repeated. 'That means he's been dead for five weeks, doesn't it?'

'Yes, I think so.'

'Then we've still got time.'

The others looked at him in confusion.

'Six weeks is the cut-off point,' he announced with an air of triumph.

'The cut-off point for what?' Otto asked.

'For raising someone from the dead,' Maximillian Hawksmoor replied.

'Raising someone from the dead!' Otto's

mother repeated. She got to her feet. 'Now listen to me, Mr Hawksmoor,' she declared. 'This whole thing has gone too far. Much too far. Against my better judgement I've allowed Otto to get mixed up in this whole magical detection business because I understand that there's magic in his blood. And I didn't want to be the one to stand between him and his destiny. And I know I'm not his real mother.'

Otto opened his mouth to protest but she silenced him with a look. 'As I say, I know I'm not his real mother but I'm still responsible for his safety – and for Juliet's too while her parents are away. And I'm telling you that raising people from the dead is going altogether too far. I know that you mean well and that you've saved all our lives in the past, but I am not having Otto and Juliet getting mixed up in something like...'

That was as far as she got. Maximillian Hawksmoor raised his hand, made a series of passes and muttered something under his breath and Mrs Spinoza froze in the middle of her sentence.

'What have you done to my mother?' Otto demanded.

'I've just put a deep relaxation spell on her, that's all,' Maximillian replied. 'She'll stay like that until I release her but she'll be perfectly OK. I promise. I had to do it, Otto,' he added when Otto continued to look at him with concern. 'I had no choice. If we don't stop Lucas Mendicant and Madame Sikursky they're liable to destroy the entire world.'

Otto nodded. 'I suppose you're right – but what about my mum? We can't leave her like this.'

'Of course not,' Maximillian agreed. He reached out and gently closed Mrs Spinoza's eyelids with his finger tips. 'Help me sit her down,' he told Otto.

Fortunately Mrs Spinoza was a small, slight woman. Between them Otto and Maximillian had no difficulty lowering her gently onto the sofa in a sitting position.

'Right,' Maximillian said when they were finished. He consulted his wristwatch. 'If we leave now we should get to Harford cemetery around midnight, which will be perfect. By the way, Otto, does your mother keep any alcohol in the flat?'

'Alcohol?' Otto said. 'I don't think this is the time to start drinking.'

'It's not for me,' Maximillian said impatiently. 'To summon a departed spirit you need to offer them something they are familiar with and might be attracted to. Runsiman was a diplomat. He spent half his life at parties and official functions. He probably drank like a fish.'

Otto thought about it. As far as he knew his mother never drank alcohol but she always poured brandy on the Christmas pudding and set it alight. 'I'll have a look in the kitchen,' he said.

He came back a few minutes later with a half-full bottle of French brandy. 'Will this do?' he asked.

Maximillian examined the label. 'Cognac!' he said. 'The perfect spirit for raising a spirit. Come on then, what are we waiting for?'

6

RAISING THE DEAD

Out in the street there was no sign of Maximillian's sporty little car.

'What's happened to your car?' Otto asked.

Maximillian smiled. 'I thought it was best to camouflage my car at the same time as the bookshop. This way.' He led them towards an ancient, and dreadfully unstylish vehicle that sat rusting quietly by the side of the road.

'You're going to drive us to Harford in that?' Otto said.

'Don't worry,' Maximillian assured him. 'It's just the bodywork that's changed. Underneath the bonnet it's the same car.'

Otto and Juliet looked doubtful but they climbed into the back and perched uncomfortably on the torn and lumpy seats. Otto half expected the vehicle to backfire and fall to pieces like a clown's car in a circus. But it started perfectly when Maximillian turned the key in the ignition and they set off to Harford at considerable speed.

'Are we going to dig up Benjamin Runsiman's coffin?' Juliet asked as they quickly left Bridlington Chawley behind. She liked to think of herself as a reasonably brave person, but the prospect of disinterring the body of someone who had been dead for five weeks filled her with dread. What kind of a state would the corpse be in?

Maximillian laughed. 'Good heavens, no!' he said. 'For one thing, I haven't got a spade in the car and I don't think we'd get very far using our bare hands.'

She breathed a sigh of relief. 'So what *are* we going to do then?'

'We're going to summon his spirit.'

'Where exactly are we summoning it from?' Otto asked. In his mind a picture was starting to form of Benjamin Runsiman in a sea of flames surrounded by devils armed with pitchforks.

'Well I can't say for certain because I haven't actually been dead myself,' Maximillian replied. 'But from what I've read spirits wait to be judged in a place called Limbo.'

'What's it like?' Juliet asked.

'Nobody really knows but one magician who claimed to have visited the place described it as a bit like waiting for a bus in a foreign country in a very thick fog without any money in your pocket to pay the fare,' Maximillian told her.

'That doesn't sound like much fun,' Juliet said. 'Perhaps that's why people say ghosts go around moaning all the time.'

'What if he doesn't want to be summoned?' Otto asked. 'He might turn nasty.'

Maximillian shook his head. 'I don't think that's very likely,' he said. 'It will probably be the most interesting thing that's happened to him since he died. But we can't be certain he won't turn up in bad company. I did read about the case of a magician who was torn to pieces by angry demons when he summoned his old school teacher and didn't get the spell quite right. But that was hundreds of years ago, so I don't think we need to worry.'

'Oh great!' Otto muttered. 'That's *so* reassuring.'

The village of Harford was about sixty miles from Bridlington Chawley and most of the journey was along narrow, winding country lanes. Despite what Maximillian had said about the car being essentially unchanged, the suspension seemed to have deteriorated badly. They were rattled and shaken about so much they began to feel queasy.

'The car is perfectly all right, actually,' Maximillian informed them when Otto complained. 'It's just a very clever spell, you see. It creates the illusion of terrible suspension to match the appearance. So you're not really uncomfortable at all; you just think you are.'

'Oh that makes me feel much better,' Otto said. He wound down the window and put his head out, gratefully breathing in the cold night air.

He was immensely relieved when they finally pulled up beside the ancient graveyard that lay in the shadow of Harford Parish Church. As Maximillian had predicted, it was not long before midnight.

Although Harford was only a little village, its inhabitants had been buried in this place for centuries. The trio stood at the cemetery gates and gazed silently at row upon row of graves.

'Don't tell me we have to look at every one of

those headstones to find Benjamin Runsiman's grave,' Otto said. 'We could be here all night.'

Maximillian shook his head. 'There won't be a headstone. Benjamin Runsiman has only been buried five weeks. You have to wait much longer for the ground to settle before you can erect a headstone.'

'So what are we going to do?'

'We're going to construct an improvised ghost compass.' Maximillian said. 'Hold the torch for me.'

While Otto held the torch, Maximillian put his hand in this pocket and pulled out a perfectly ordinary compass. Then he passed his hand over it several times whispering a spell too quietly for the other two to make out any of the words. At first nothing happened, then the needle twitched and began spinning furiously before coming to a halt once more. Maximillian looked satisfied. He put his hand in his pocket again and took out a piece of paper. Otto and Juliet saw that it was a print out of the photograph of Benjamin Runsiman they had discovered on the web.

'Look at the picture,' Maximillian told them. 'Concentrate on the image. Try to hold it in your mind. Now touch the compass with one finger.'

Otto and Juliet did as he said. Immediately the compass needle swung towards the south-east.

'Right, let's get going,' Maximillian said.

The graveyard was a shifting pattern of silvery moonlight and menacing shadow as they threaded their way through the tombstones. In the distance a vixen screeched, a call that seemed so human it made the hairs on the back of Otto's neck stand on end and from all around them came mysterious rustling noises.

After a while they reached the part of the cemetery where the newer graves were situated. Maximillian came to a halt and they repeated the procedure with the compass. This time the needle pointed directly east. They turned in that direction and presently came to an unmarked plot where the earth was piled a little higher than the level of the surrounding ground.

'This could be it,' Maximillian declared.

They tried the compass once more and this time the needle began spinning furiously.

'Bingo!' Maximillian said. He consulted his wristwatch. 'And it's exactly five minutes till midnight. Perfect timing. Let's get cracking.'

He took the bottle of cognac out of his bag along with four black candles and two boxes of matches. 'At least it's not raining,' he said. 'It's a nightmare trying to light candles in the rain.' He gave two candles each to Otto and Juliet. 'Plant them at the four corners of the grave but don't light them until I tell you,' he instructed.

Then he stood in front of the grave, raised both his arms in the air and began chanting in a loud voice. Amid the torrent of outlandish syllables Otto distinctly heard the diplomat's name repeated several times.

After a few minutes Maximillian dropped his hands and nodded to Otto and Juliet to light the four black candles. He picked up the bottle of brandy and poured it into the earth in the centre of the grave. At first nothing happened and Otto began to wonder whether they had been wasting their time. Then he noticed that the temperature had dropped considerably and he shivered. A moment later his skin began to itch.

A sudden gust of wind tore at the candle flames, making them dance crazily, but somehow they stayed alight. In the air above the grave a column of mist began to form, growing more and more solid, until at last it took the form of Benjamin Runsiman.

He looked exactly as he did in the photograph. The only difference was that instead of a tuxedo he was wearing striped pyjamas. Otto wasn't sure how he'd been expecting the diplomat to be dressed – in a white sheet perhaps. Certainly not pyjamas. But he remembered that Benjamin Runsiman had been murdered in his bed. Presumably these were the last clothes he had worn.

'Who dares summon me to this dreadful place?' Benjamin Runsiman demanded, shivering and hugging himself, as if he felt the cold quite as much as Otto did.

'Maximillian Hawksmoor at your service, Mr Runsiman. These are my associates, Otto Spinoza and Juliet Pennington.'

'How do you do?' Otto said.

'Pleased to meet you,' Juliet echoed.

'What is the meaning of this?' the spirit demanded crossly. 'I happened to be in the middle of a meeting.'

'We apologise most sincerely for interrupting

you, Mr Runsiman,' Maximillian told him, 'but we have a very important proposition to put to you.'

'Important proposition? What are you talking about?' Benjamin Runsiman managed to summon up as much dignity as a spirit dressed in pyjamas could possibly possess. 'There's nothing you could possibly offer that might interest me. I'm dead. Deceased. Finished with your world. Don't you understand that? And good riddance! That's what I say!'

Maximillian looked unmoved by the spirit's angry speech. 'I understand that it is five weeks since you were killed,' he said, 'and according to everything I've read, that means you will shortly be appearing before The Authority, for judgement. Would I be right in this assumption?'

'I don't see what business that is of yours,' the spirit replied frostily.

'It's true though, isn't it?' Maximillian continued, unperturbed. 'You're waiting to be judged.'

Benjamin Runsiman opened his mouth to speak but before he could utter a word, a second spirit materialised beside him – a suave looking man in an elegant three-piece suit. He immediately turned to Benjamin Runsiman, raised his index finger in warning and said, 'Don't answer that!'

'Who are you?' Maximillian demanded.

'Allow me to introduce myself,' the newcomer declared. ' My name is Mr Grigori of Lucifer, Mephistopheles and Beelzebub Limited. I am Mr Runsiman's legal representative in the after-life.'

Maximillian sighed. 'A lawyer! I might have known.' He turned back to Benjamin Runsiman. 'So *this* is who you've been hanging around with since you departed,' he said. 'It won't do you any good, you know.'

'Take no notice of that remark!' Grigori ordered.

'He's only after your soul,' Maximillian went on. 'Can't you see that?'

'And what exactly are *you* after?' Grigori demanded, his voice dripping with contempt.

Maximillian refused to even look at Grigori. Instead he addressed himself directly to the former diplomat. 'We're here because we need your help, Mr Runsiman,' he began. 'I don't mind admitting that. But we're also offering you the chance to do one good deed before your case comes up for judgement. Think about what that might mean for the rest of your afterlife.'

'Good deed, my foot!' Grigori declared angrily. 'They want information, that's all.'

'Your so-called adviser is quite correct,' Maximillian went on. 'Information is what we want, information about Lucas Mendicant, the man who was responsible for your murder. Why should you protect him?'

Benjamin Runsiman looked thoughtful.

'You don't have to answer that,' Grigori interjected.

'Help us track him down and you'd be helping yourself at the same time,' Maximillian went on. 'Because you know what they're going to ask when your judgement comes up, don't you? Have you done a single good deed in your entire life? That's what they'll want to know. And – have you?'

Benjamin Runsiman looked thoughtful.

'Tell him, no comment,' Grigori ordered.

'Just as I thought,' Maximillian said. 'You can't think of a single thing, can you? Not one good deed in a whole lifetime. You know where you're going to end up, don't you? Unless you take this one chance to tip the scales in your favour.'

'Don't listen to him,' Grigori insisted. 'He doesn't know what he's talking about. These are legal matters. You need proper professional advice and if you want my opinion—'

Suddenly Benjamin Runsiman swung round and confronted Grigori angrily. 'I *don't* want your opinion!' he said. 'Ever since I died you've been pestering me and I'm sick of it. You know what I'm beginning to think? I reckon you've been whispering in my ear for most of my life. I've been taking your advice without even realising it. And what good did it do me?'

'You were a very successful diplomat,' Grigori pointed out.

'Maybe I was. But I was also a miserable human being who ended up getting strangled in his pyjamas by a man he thought was his friend. What kind of a life do you call that?' He looked Grigori directly in the eye. 'No comment to make, I suppose? What a surprise. Well, you know what? You can go to hell as far as I'm concerned.'

Grigori winced. 'You'll regret that!' he said. And with a furious look he disappeared.

'What a relief!' Benjamin Runsiman said turning to the others. 'So, what exactly do you want to know about Lucas Mendicant?'

'Do you know where he is hiding?' Maximillian asked.

'Oh, that's easy enough,' the spirit replied. 'Lucas Mendicant is an honoured guest of the Kabolim of Omustakah.'

Maximillian's face fell. 'Are you sure about that?'

'Quite sure. He told me himself just before he strangled me. Now if that is all you wish to know, I think I'll be on my way. If you wouldn't mind…' He looked at Maximillian expectantly.

Maximillian nodded. 'Of course,' he said. 'I dismiss you.'

'Good luck with the judgement!' Otto called out.

But the spirit of Benjamin Runsiman had already disappeared and with a gust of cold air the four black candles went out.

Maximillian sighed. 'Well, we've got what we came for,' he said. 'Let's get out of here.'

'Who did he say Lucas Mendicant was a guest of?' Otto asked as they made their way back towards the cemetery gates.

'The Kabolim,' Maximillian told him. 'He is the ruler of Omustakah, a tiny kingdom in the Great Northern Mountains of Quillipoth.'

'That's good, isn't it?' Otto said. 'I mean, now that we know where he's hiding, all we have to do is go after him and get the tablet back. Right?'

'I'm afraid it's not going to be that easy,' Maximillian said. 'For one thing, Omustakah is a savage place, even by elemental standards. They're very fond of chopping people's heads off. For another, getting to Omustakah is going to be much harder than you realise.'

'But can't we use the fountain?' Juliet asked. The previous summer they had discovered that a disused fountain in the grounds of a stately home in Bridlington Chawley was a magical portal between their world and the elemental world of Quillipoth.

'The fountain only takes you to one place in Quillipoth, the city of Abirkadash,' Maximillian told her. 'That's about as far from Omustakah as Australia is from England.'

'Can't you reset the coordinates or something?' Otto asked.

'I'm afraid not. Magic isn't like a satellite

navigation system,' Maximillian replied. 'It needs something to work on.'

'What sort of thing?'

Maximillian shrugged. 'It could be anything really, just so long as it once belonged to Lucas Mendicant, but the more personal the item, the better.'

'What about the university where he used to work?' Otto suggested. 'There might be something there that we could use.'

'Good idea!' Maximillian said. 'But right now we need to go back to the bookshop and get some sleep. It's been a long day and it'll probably be an even longer one tomorrow.'

The journey back to Bridlington Chawley seemed to take hours. Otto and Juliet were both struggling to stay awake by the time they pulled up outside the bookshop, or at least outside the spot where the bookshop ought to be, for the magical camouflage was still doing its job.

'At least there's no sign of Mr Jones's men,' Otto said, glancing up and down the street warily.

'Perhaps they've given up,' Juliet suggested.

'People like Mr Jones never give up,' Maximillian observed gloomily. 'Come on, let's get inside while there's no one around. Remember, you have to turn your back on the shop and look over your left shoulder.'

They did as he said and there was the bookshop, just as it had always been.

'If anyone saw us they'd think we were mad,' Otto said with a grin, as the three of them shuffled crab-like towards the shop. But the humour of the situation soon began to wear thin as he struggled to get the key in a lock which he could neither see nor reach properly. At last he succeeded and almost fell through the doorway with weariness.

Otto's mother was still sitting in exactly the same position as they had left her. Otto got a blanket from the bedroom and draped it gently over her shoulders. 'I'm really sorry about this, Mum,' he said.

'I think it would be best if we all spent the night here in the same room,' Maximillian suggested. 'In case Mr Jones finds a way to bypass the magical camouflage and decides to mount some kind of raid.'

'Good idea!' Otto said. He had been secretly dreading Maximillian driving off and leaving them to fend for themselves. He went into the bedroom and brought out all the bedding he could carry. They spread sheets on the floor, then the three of them took off their shoes and lay down fully-clothed, covering themselves with duvets and blankets. Within minutes they were all fast asleep.

Outside, the streets of Bridlington Chawley were silent and empty except for a solitary white van that cruised back and forth over the same small network of streets. Its two burly passengers stared at a map in confusion and the driver, smartly dressed but also burly, called them all sorts of names, none of which were at all polite.

7

THE LOVESICK SECRETARY

The city of Haverstock had been built at the base of a valley and you could see it from the road long before you reached it. The outskirts looked just like any other city with high rise buildings, warehouses and retail parks. But nestling at the heart of Haverstock was the medieval town and the ancient university buildings all built of the same yellowish stone. Their ornamented spires, turrets and domes were gleaming in the early morning sunlight, making them look like some enormous and elaborate cake.

As they made their way towards the city centre Maximillian told Otto and Juliet all about the university. He had been a student there himself, many years ago, he explained. Maximillian's exact age was something that Otto had tried, without success, to discover. Maximillian himself was always vague when you asked him directly, insisting that he had lost count of his birthdays.

'Haverstock University is one of England's top five tourist attractions,' Maximillian said as they drove through the narrow side streets looking for somewhere to park. Even at this early hour, the streets were thronged with tourists, busily taking photographs of each other as they posed in front of the historic gateways.

At last Maximillian found somewhere to leave the car and they set off for the office of the Dean who had once been Maximillian's old tutor. 'Nobody at the university likes talking about Lucas Mendicant,' Maximillian warned them, 'because he attracted so much bad publicity when he disappeared with all that money. I phoned the Dean and told him you're my niece and nephew and that I've brought you here to show you around. So, for today, don't forget, I'm Uncle Max.'

Though the Dean's office was situated in the grandest of all the university buildings, his room was surprisingly small and plainly furnished with just a large desk, an expensive-looking Turkish carpet and an awful lot of bookshelves.

The Dean rose to meet them as they entered. He was a tall man with a slight stoop, as if he were permanently afraid of banging his head. He had crooked teeth, a great deal of untidy white hair and he wore a suit that looked as if he had been living in it for the last thirty years. Not really a great advertisement for university life, Otto decided.

The Dean looked enormously pleased to see Maximillian, taking his hand and shaking it enthusiastically. 'Wonderful to see you again, Max. One of my very best students. And this is your niece and nephew. Splendid! Splendid! Well I hope you're going to take after your uncle, that's all. Now then, do sit down. Make yourselves at home.'

Making yourself at home wasn't easy when the chairs were hard and a bit rickety. For the next fifteen minutes Maximillian and the Dean talked about people they had both known while Otto and Juliet tried not to look completely bored.

The Dean would say, 'What about that fellow Corballis – you know the one who spoke all those languages – what's he doing now?' and Maximillian would tell him that Corballis was writing a book on the history of the toothpick in Ancient Persia or something equally obscure and then the Dean would nod and say, 'Splendid! Splendid!' and move on to someone else. But eventually Maximillian managed to get his old tutor onto the subject of Lucas Mendicant.

The Dean's face collapsed into an expression of utter misery. 'Dreadful business!' he said. 'Absolutely dreadful! All that money, and then reporters crawling all over the college, asking questions, taking photographs. Couldn't get anything done for months.'

'No one suspected him, I suppose?' Maximillian said.

'That's just it,' the Dean exclaimed. 'We all thought he was a marvellous chap. First rate scholar. Been to the very best schools. Turns out he was an absolute scoundrel. Couldn't believe it. We even threw a party for him, you know, to celebrate raising all that money. Balloons, cakes, sherry. That sort of thing. There we were, all standing round waiting like a lot of five-year-olds at a nursery – it was going to be a surprise you see – but of course he didn't show up. Instead, in walks a policeman who says they've found his car abandoned in the middle of the countryside. At first we thought something terrible must have happened to him, but then we discovered that the money was gone as well and we realised he'd made fools of the lot of us. Do you know he took everything out of his office, even the furniture? Nothing left except the light bulb. That's the kind of fellow he was.'

'He didn't leave anything at all?' Maximillian said, trying not to let his disappointment show.

'Not so much as a button.'

'Who would you say knew him best?' Maximillian asked.

'Oh, that would be his secretary, Madeline Gauntlet. Terribly silly woman, I'm afraid.'

'In what way was she silly?' Otto asked.

The Dean frowned and looked at Otto as if he could not quite remember who he was for a moment. 'Um, well,' he stuttered, 'you wouldn't really understand, I'm afraid.'

'Try me,' Otto suggested.

The Dean looked astonished for a moment. He clearly wasn't used to dealing with children. Certainly not children who answered back.

'My nephew and niece are extremely sophisticated for their years,' Maximillian assured him. 'You can tell them anything.'

'Well, if you say so,' the Dean said. But he still looked uncomfortable.

'Did she have a crush on him?' Juliet asked.

'A crush!' the Dean said. 'Do you know I haven't heard that expression for years? One doesn't come across it very much in archaeological studies, of course. But yes, I think you could say that, young lady. She had a crush on him. More than a crush, really.'

'She was in love with him?' Otto said.

'Exactly. Head over heels. Like someone who'd been hypnotised, if you know what I mean.'

'I think we know exactly what you mean,' Maximillian said. 'You know, I'd really like to talk to this Ms Gauntlet.'

'What on earth for?' the Dean said. For the first time since he'd welcomed them into the room he looked suspicious. 'I do hope you're not working for the newspapers,' he said.

Maximillian smiled reassuringly. 'Of course not! I'm an old Haverstockian, remember.'

'Of course!' said the Dean. 'That's the trouble with something like this. It makes you suspicious of everybody. But I think we can rely on an old Haverstockian. So what *did* you want with her?'

'I was just interested in some of the work that Mendicant had been doing before he disappeared. He *was* one of the world's experts on Ancient Babylon, I believe.'

'Oh yes, quite,' the Dean said. 'Absolute expert. Jolly clever chap, really. We were very lucky to have him teaching here. Oh no, of course we weren't. Silly thing to say. Now then, where was I?'

'You were telling me about Madeline Gauntlet,' Maximillian reminded him.

'That's it. The lovesick secretary. I'm afraid you're out of luck. She resigned shortly after Mendicant disappeared. She said she couldn't bear to come into the university every day without seeing him.'

'Do you have an address for her?' Maximillian asked.

'She won't know anything,' the Dean insisted. 'One of the silliest women I've ever met. Followed Mendicant around all the time like a puppy. I was glad to see the back of her, to tell you the truth.'

'I'd like to have a word with her all the same,'

Maximillian said, quietly but firmly.

'Very well,' the Dean said. He rummaged around in his desk, opening drawers and taking out all sorts of things – notepads, staplers, balls of string, a single woollen glove, a screwdriver, a very ancient cheese sandwich – then putting them all back in again. After several minutes, he produced a rather grubby piece of paper that looked as if it had been torn from an exercise book. 'Here it is,' he said triumphantly.

Maximillian took the address and got to his feet. Relieved that the interview was over at last, Otto and Juliet followed suit.

The Dean looked surprised. 'Going already? I thought your niece and nephew might want a tour of the archaeology department. We've found some splendid pieces of broken pottery from Mesopotamia. Fourth century BC, we think.'

'We've seen enough, thanks,' Otto said.

'Oh well, if you're sure. But do come again some time. There's so much to talk about.'

Madeline Gauntlet lived on the outskirts of Haverstock in a shabby, semi-detached house on a modern estate. It was as different to the old-fashioned grandeur of the university buildings as it was possible to imagine.

'Are you sure he gave you the right address?' Otto asked as they gazed at the abandoned garden, full of weeds and litter. The drawn curtains made the house look very unwelcoming. 'This place looks as if it's been empty for ages.'

'We might as well give it a try,' Maximillian remarked.

They walked up to the front door and rang the bell.

There was no answer but Otto thought he saw the curtains twitch ever so slightly upstairs. 'Ring again,' he suggested.

Maximillian pressed the bell and let it ring for ages this time. Finally, when they were on the point of giving up, the door was suddenly pulled opened and a very thin woman in a pink nylon dressing gown and matching slippers peered out at them, blinking repeatedly as if she did not often see the light of day.

'Sorry to disturb you,' Maximillian began. 'We're looking for Madeline Gauntlet.'

'I am Madeline Gauntlet,' the woman said in a voice so faint they could barely hear her.

'I wonder if we could have a word with you,' Maximillian said.

'Not really,' she replied, sounding as if the effort of speaking was almost too much for her. 'I'm really much too busy. Ever so many things to do.' With that she began to close the door.

'It's about Lucas Mendicant,' Otto said quickly.

The door opened again. 'Lucas Mendicant?' It was as if a light had been switched on behind her eyes. 'Have they found him?' she asked. 'Is he all right? Did he say anything? Did he mention me?' She was getting more and more excited by the second. 'Where is he? Please tell me. I must go and see him. I must—'

Maximillian held a hand up to stop her. 'Hold on a minute, Ms Gauntlet,' he said. 'I'm afraid we haven't come to tell you that he's been found.'

She slumped visibly at this news, like a deflated balloon.

'But we would like to talk to you about him, if you could spare us a few minutes of your time.'

'Are you from the newspapers?'

Maximillian handed her one of his business cards.

She frowned. 'The Magical Detective Agency?'

'At your service,' he said with a beaming smile. 'I am Maximillian Hawksmoor and these are my two associates.'

Madeline Gauntlet looked suspiciously at Otto and Juliet. 'They're only children,' she said.

'Children make the best detectives,' Maximillian told her. 'They notice far more than adults.'

Madeline Gauntlet looked unconvinced, but she shrugged. 'OK then, come in,' she said.

The first thing Otto saw when he stepped into the hallway was Lucas Mendicant. There were photographs of him everywhere. A picture at the bottom of the stairs showed the disgraced professor beaming happily at the camera as someone presented him with a huge cheque, like a lottery winner. Otto studied Mendicant's face. He was undoubtedly a good-looking man and even from this picture you could tell that he had charm – but there was something about his eyes that gave away his real personality. He looked far too pleased with himself. Like a corrupt politician who has just won an election.

Madeline Gauntlet ushered them into her sitting room. There were many more pictures of Mendicant in here. A huge one over the sofa showed him with his arm around Ms Gauntlet. He had the same politician's smile on his face whereas she looked as if she was in a state of complete ecstasy.

'He didn't do it, you know,' she said when they were all sitting down. 'Steal the money, I mean. I told that to the reporters. I said Lucas would never do a thing like that.'

'So what do you think happened to him?' Maximillian asked.

'He was kidnapped.'

'Why do you say that?'

'Because he would never have left of his own free will, not without letting me know. He told me everything.'

Otto thought this sounded extremely unlikely.

'You and Mr Mendicant were very close then?' Maximillian said.

Without warning Ms Gauntlet burst into tears. 'He was the only man I ever loved,' she sobbed. She took an embroidered handkerchief out of the pocket of her dressing gown and dabbed at her eyes. 'I'm sorry,' she said. 'It's just that he meant everything in the world to me. And now that he's gone my life is completely empty.'

Much more of this and I'm going to throw up, Otto thought to himself.

But Maximillian nodded sympathetically. 'I understand how you feel,' he said.

Madeline Gauntlet put away her handkerchief. 'Have you ever been in love, Mr Hawksmoor?'

'Not exactly in love,' Maximillian replied. 'But I'm very fond of lemon sherbets.'

Ms Gauntlet frowned. 'Whatever do you mean?' she asked.

'Oh nothing,' Maximillian said. 'I've been told he took everything from his office. Is that right?'

'He didn't take it,' Ms Gauntlet said angrily. 'They did.'

'They?'

'The people who kidnapped him.'

'Oh yes, of course,' Maximillian said, 'the people who kidnapped him.'

'They had to get rid of all the evidence, you see,' Ms Gauntlet continued. 'They wanted people to think that he'd run away with the money.'

'Yes, of course they did,' Maximillian said. 'What dreadful people they must be! But what I was wondering was whether you had anything that had once belonged to Mr Mendicant, something that might help lead us to him.'

Madeline Gauntlet shook her head. 'They took everything,' she said. 'All I've got left is my memories and a piece of his tooth.'

'I'm sorry,' Maximillian said. 'Did you say a piece of his tooth?'

Madeline Gauntlet nodded. 'It broke off when he was eating a toffee. He spat it out into the waste paper bin but I rescued it afterwards.'

Otto and Juliet exchanged glasses. They didn't need to say anything. Their looks made it clear exactly what they thought of Madeline Gauntlet. Completely and utterly bonkers!

'So you've still got this piece of tooth?' Maximillian said.

'Oh yes,' Ms Gauntlet replied, 'I sleep with it under my pillow every night.'

'I wonder if you would consider lending it to us?' Maximillian asked.

'Lending it to you!' She looked outraged. 'Certainly not! That's all I've got left of him.'

'It could be very helpful in tracking him down.'

Madeline Gauntlet got to her feet. 'I think this interview has gone far enough. I must ask you to leave. Immediately.'

Otto, Juliet and Maximillian stood up.

'We didn't mean to upset you, Ms Gauntlet,' Juliet began.

But Madeline Gauntlet had stopped listening. 'For all I know you could be working with his kidnappers,' she said.

'I can assure you we're not,' Maximillian said.

'That's what you say. But you wanted to get your hands on the tooth, didn't you? Get out of my house immediately!'

Otto, Juliet and Maximillian made their way swiftly to the front door. There was a dangerous look on Madeline Gauntlet's face. Otto had the feeling that she could turn into a knife-wielding maniac in the blink of an eye.

'You're as bad as the journalists,' she yelled

when they were finally outside. Give us an interview, give us a picture, give us a quote, that's what they said. Over and over again. And now you want me to give you the tooth as well. Well you can't have it, do you hear? You'll have to kill me first!'

And with that she slammed the door in their faces.

'Wow!' Otto said. 'That woman is a total psycho.'

Maximillian nodded. 'She's highly unstable, there's no doubt about it. All the same, we have to get that tooth.'

Otto and Juliet looked at him in horror. 'You can't be serious,' Otto said. 'You heard what she said. We'd have to kill her.'

'Except she might kill us first,' Juliet pointed out.

'Yes, yes, I know that,' Maximillian said, 'but it doesn't make a blind bit of difference. We have to get the tooth and that's all there is to it. We need a plan. Let's go and sit in the car and think.'

They got back into Maximillian's car and he handed round a packet of sherbet lemons. They took one each and for some time there was nothing but the sound of contented sucking. Finally, Otto spoke.

'The way I see it is this,' he said. 'Madeline Gauntlet is not going to give us the tooth willingly.'

'Agreed,' Maximillian said.

'So there's only one option open to us: we have to steal it.'

Juliet shook her head. 'Stealing is wrong,' she said.

'It's only a tooth,' Otto pointed out.

'Only a fragment of a tooth, actually,' Maximillian added.

'It doesn't matter,' Juliet said. 'That tooth represents her love for Lucas Mendicant. And that's the only thing she's got left in the world. We can't take it away from her.'

Maximillian sighed. 'You're right,' he said. He handed round the sherbet lemons again.

'Wait a minute!' Otto said suddenly, 'What if we replace it with another bit of tooth when she's not looking? She won't even know it's gone. We won't have stolen anything from her. She'll still believe she has a bit of Lucas Mendicant under her pillow.'

'That's brilliant, Otto,' Maximillian said.

'There's just one snag. Where are we supposed to get another bit of tooth?'

'Actually, I might have the answer to that,' Juliet said.

8

OPERATION TOOTH FAIRY

Belsham Manor was a large stately home on the outskirts of Bridlington Chawley. The grounds were surrounded by a high brick wall and the only entrance was through an enormous pair of iron gates that were left permanently open. Maximillian drove up to those gates and stopped the car.

'You know what to do?' he asked.

'Of course,' Juliet replied.

'Good. We'll be back as soon as we can,' he told her. 'And remember, stay out of sight while you're waiting for me.' With that he drove through the manor gates while Juliet moved out of sight behind a tree.

Inside the gates, the driveway continued for a short way, bordered on either side by dense evergreen hedges before coming to a fork. One branch led to Belsham Manor, and the other to The Lodge, the house that Juliet lived in with her parents. From this position it was possible to see both buildings clearly. Just as Maximillian had expected, a white van was parked outside The Lodge. One of Mr Jones' men was standing beside it smoking a cigarette. He was looking in the opposite direction and had not yet seen Maximillian's car.

As quietly as possible, Maximillian turned his car round. Then he sounded his horn several times. The thug's head swivelled round. Maximillian stuck his head out of the window and waved. The thug threw away his cigarette and made a dash for the van.

'Well, that seems to have got his attention,' Maximillian said. 'Now for the exciting part!' He accelerated out of the gates like a racing driver. A few moments later the white van followed, hot on his trail.

Watching from behind the tree, Juliet waited until the white van was completely out of sight before walking briskly through the gates and up to her house. She let herself in with her key and went straight upstairs to her parents' bedroom.

On the top of her parents' wardrobe was an old shoe box in which her mother kept mementoes from when Juliet was a baby. Juliet stood on a chair to lift the box down from the wardrobe, blew away the dust and lifted the lid. Inside were photographs of a tiny baby lying in a cot. Juliet had seen these pictures before and found it hard to believe that this helpless infant was really herself. But there was no time for thoughts like that. She went systematically through the contents of the box, lifting out the plastic identification bracelet the hospital had put on her wrist to stop her getting mixed up with all the other babies, her first pair of shoes, a baby's dummy, a battered pink rabbit. Ah! There it was, a little cloth bag tied at the mouth with string. She loosened the string and poured the contents out onto the palm of her hand. There were about six small, yellowish teeth. Hers.

Juliet wondered whether her mother was especially weird or whether this was the sort of thing all parents did. But she would probably never find out since it wasn't really the sort of thing you could ask your friends at school. 'Oh by the way, I was just wondering whether your mother kept a collection of your old baby teeth?'

She chose the smallest tooth from the

collection and put the rest back in the bag. Then she put everything back in the box and replaced it on top of the wardrobe.

She looked out of the window before going back downstairs and letting herself out. No point in taking any chances! Fortunately there was no sign of the white van.

While Juliet had been locating a tooth, Otto had been trying to decide whether he should be impressed or simply terrified by Maximillian's driving. They were tearing through the narrow country lanes at blood-curdling speed and screeching round bends, spraying gravel and mud in all directions.

'Where on earth did you learn to drive like this?' Otto asked.

'I went through a rebellious phase when I was a young man,' Maximillian told him. 'My father was so keen for me to be a magician that it brought out a stubborn streak in me. I became a professional racing driver instead. Absolutely loved it! Of course magic called me back in the end. But not before I picked up a few tricks. Like this one. Hold on tight!'

Without slowing down, Maximillian

wrenched the wheel to one side and pulled on the handbrake. The car spun round to the left and they hurtled into a narrow side road so completely obscured by overhanging trees that Otto had not even realised it was there. Maximillian cut the engine and they waited in silence. A few moments later Mr Jones' men shot past.

Maximillian chuckled. 'They're not very good, are they?'

'Maybe. But it won't take them long to realise what's happened, will it?' Otto pointed out.

'Very true.' Maximillian started up the car once more. 'We must go back and collect Juliet.'

Juliet was waiting behind the tree where they had left her. She got in the car and held up the tooth to show them. 'Now comes the hard bit,' Maximillian said. 'Swapping your tooth for Lucas Mendicant's.'

'Do you have a plan?' Juliet asked.

'Well, sort of,' Maximillian said. 'I thought we'd wait until nightfall and then break into the house.'

'Is that it?' Otto asked. 'It's not much of a plan, is it? She sleeps with that tooth under her pillow, remember.'

'I know,' Maximillian said, 'but I still think it's our best chance. If we try to approach the house in daylight and she spots us, she'll go crazy. Anything could happen.'

'So what do we do for the rest of the day?' Otto asked.

'We're going shopping,' Maximillian replied.

'Shopping? What for?'

'Warm clothes. Didn't I mention that Omustakah is very cold?'

Otto and Juliet both shook their heads. 'No, you didn't,' Otto said.

'How cold is very cold?' Otto asked.

'About as cold as Russia in winter,' Maximillian told them.

'Oh, great!' Otto said.

They drove back to Haverstock and spent the day stocking up on anoraks, boots, hats, scarves, gloves, socks and anything else they could think of that might keep out the cold. Maximillian paid for everything. 'Don't worry about the cost,' he told them. 'A magician has ways of getting money when he needs it.'

Even after they had bought everything they needed as well as an awful lot of stuff they probably didn't need, there was still a lot of time to kill. So they got themselves take-away pizzas and sat in Maximillian's car at the end of Madeleine Gauntlet's road, waiting for darkness to fall and then waiting even longer until the lights upstairs in Ms Gauntlet's house went out.

'We'll give her another half hour to go to sleep, then it's Operation Tooth Fairy,' Maximillian said.

'Let's just hope she isn't an insomniac,' Otto added.

Thirty minutes later the trio got out of Maximillian's car and walked in the direction of Madeleine Gauntlet's house, keeping as much as possible to the shadows. On one side Ms Gauntlet's house was joined to the neighbouring house but on the other there was a passage that led round the side towards the back garden. The way was blocked by a wooden door.

Maximillian Hawksmoor reached over the top of the door and felt about with his hand.

'Got it,' he said. 'Just a simple bolt. Not very security conscious, is she?' He slid back the bolt, pushed the door open and they made their way to the back of the house.

'Now we need to find an unlocked window,'

Maximillian said. He took a torch out of his pocket and began to try the ground floor windows systematically. They were all locked except for one very small casement in the kitchen. Otto shook his head. 'We'll never get through there,' he said.

'*I* might,' Juliet volunteered. 'Give me the torch. And a leg up.'

Maximillian passed her the torch, then he and Otto cupped their hands together, allowing Juliet to step onto them.

'When you're inside, open the door and let me in,' Maximillian said. 'I'll do the burgling.'

Slowly and carefully, Juliet began wiggling her way through the window. It was a very tight fit and she was trying to avoid making any noise. When she was halfway through she put out her hands, located the draining board of the sink and allowed the rest of her body to follow her in. The difficult bit was getting her legs through without falling head first but she managed it somehow, ending up sitting in the sink. She was wet and undignified, but she was in.

On the other side of the window she could see Maximillian pointing towards the back door. She shook her head. She was smaller than he was and lighter on her feet. If anyone was going to succeed in getting the tooth from under Madeline Gauntlet's pillow then it had to be her.

She climbed down from the sink and tiptoed out into the hallway where she waited for some time, listening, just in case Ms Gauntlet had heard anything. But there was no sound of any movement upstairs.

Very slowly, she began climbing the stairs, trying to keep her steps as close as possible to the wall. She had heard once that this was the part of a staircase least likely to creak. At the top of the stairs she was confronted by three doors, all closed. She was pretty sure that Ms Gauntlet was in the front bedroom. That was where the light had gone on and then off while they sat in Maximillian's car, waiting. The other two must be the bathroom and a spare bedroom.

She crept up to the door of the front bedroom and put her ear to the door. Someone was snoring inside. Juliet very much hoped that it was Ms Gauntlet and that she was alone. She gripped the door handle and turned it as slowly and silently as she was able. There was a click and the door opened. Juliet put her head round and cautiously shone the torch inside the room.

The front bedroom was dominated by an enormous four-poster bed that looked as though it had come from some medieval castle. Lying on the bed surrounded by pillows and teddy bears was the person responsible for the snoring which was considerably louder once you were actually inside the room. There was no doubt that it was Madeline Gauntlet.

Juliet crept over to the bed and knelt down beside it. Under which of the many pillows would she find Lucas Mendicant's tooth? Keeping her eye on Ms Gauntlet's prostrate figure all the time, Juliet slid her hand under the pillow nearest her. There was nothing underneath it.

One by one she tried the other pillows. All the while Ms Gauntlet's snoring was growing louder and louder. Suddenly, the woman gave a ferocious snort that an African warthog would have been proud of. She seemed on the brink of waking up. Juliet froze, holding her breath but then Ms Gauntlet relaxed and her regular pattern of snoring resumed. Juliet breathed out slowly. By now she had tried every pillow except the one on which Ms Gauntlet's head was resting. I might have known it would be that one, Juliet thought to herself.

As carefully as if she was putting her hand in a cage with a poisonous snake, Juliet began to slide her hand under the final pillow. Ms Gauntlet mumbled something that sounded like, 'Lucas, I love you,' and turned in the bed, trapping Juliet's hand firmly under the pillow.

But though she did not dare move, Juliet was triumphant for she had felt something small and hard under that pillow. It had to be the tooth! Her fingers clasped around it and she began trying to withdraw her hand as gently as possible.

It was at this point that things started to go wrong. Juliet became aware of a feeling of warmth on one side of her chest. No, not just warmth – heat. It felt as though some part of her clothing was on fire. She looked down and saw that the badge of Corny that was pinned to the lapel of her jacket was glowing in the dark, as brightly as if it were a light bulb, and she remembered what Maximillian had told her – the spell he had used on Corny would wear off by itself sooner or later.

'Not now!' Juliet thought to herself. 'Please not now!'

But even as she said these things there was a dazzling flash of light and suddenly instead of a brooch, Cornelius the cat was clinging to Juliet's lapel, his eyes as wide as saucers, his fur standing on end. He gave a great meow of bewilderment and leapt backwards landing fairly and squarely on Madeleine Gauntlet's head.

Madeleine Gauntlet sat up in bed and screamed. Cornelius arched his back and hissed furiously at her. Juliet grabbed the tooth then slid under the bed, hoping that somehow she had not been noticed.

A light went on, a real light this time as Madeleine Gauntlet's fingers located the switch of her beside lamp. A moment later teddy bears began hurtling across the room as she flung everything she could find in Cornelius' direction.

Juliet watched from beneath the bed in dismay as Cornelius dashed manically about the room, sending bottles of perfume and make-up flying as he leapt on top of the dressing table and from there to one of Ms Gauntlet's velvet curtains, gouging great tears in the fabric with his claws, and from the curtain to the top of the wardrobe.

By now Madeleine Gauntlet was out of her bed and she had graduated from throwing teddy bears to flinging books, stiletto heeled shoes, even an alarm clock in Cornelius' direction. And her aim was getting better all the time. Spying the half-open bedroom door, Cornelius leapt down from the top of the wardrobe and shot down the stairs with Madeleine Gauntlet in hot pursuit.

This was Juliet's chance. She took the substitute tooth out of her pocket and slid it under the pillow, then she crept out onto the landing. The chase had moved downstairs to the kitchen and she could hear the sound of plates being smashed. Somehow she had to get herself and Corny out of the house without Ms Gauntlet seeing her. But she had no idea how to go about it.

By now Cornelius was backed into a corner of the kitchen and Ms Gauntlet was advancing on him clutching a rolling pin. There was a murderous look in her eye.

It was at this point that Cornelius decided to

take matters into his own hands. Speaking in the rich, deep chocolaty voice that he had acquired when he visited the magical world of Quillipoth the previous summer, he addressed his attacker. 'Look here, madam, this is no way to behave. In fact it's downright uncivilised. Why don't you put that rolling pin down and let's talk about this in a reasonable fashion?'

Madeleine Gauntlet stopped in her tracks and the colour drained from her voice. 'A talking cat?' she said to herself. 'I'm going crazy.'

'Not at all,' Cornelius said reassuringly. 'For one thing crazy people never admit they're crazy. So, logically, that means you must be sane. Now if you would just lower that rolling pin a little, I'll explain exactly what is going on.'

Madeleine Gauntlet boggled. But she lowered the rolling pin.

'Well done!' Cornelius said. 'Now let's take this very slowly, shall we? You're standing in your kitchen in the middle of the night looking at a talking cat. It doesn't make sense, does it?'

Madeleine Gauntlet shook her head.

'So what can you think of that makes absolutely no sense but happens in the middle of the night?'

'A dream?' Madeleine Gauntlet whispered.

'Exactly!' Cornelius replied. 'And that's all this is. You're having a bad dream.'

Ms Gauntlet nodded her head slowly.

'It's the only explanation that makes sense, if you think about it,' Corny continued. 'After all, cats can't talk, can they? So obviously I'm just a figment of your imagination. Now the question is, how are you going to get out of this dream? Well I'll tell you how. Just put that rolling pin down on the draining board.'

Madeleine Gauntlet did as she was instructed.

'Wonderful! Now turn round and go back up the stairs to bed. It's as simple as that.'

Juliet had been standing at the top of the stairs listening to this exchange. Now she ducked into the bathroom and closed the door behind her, leaving just a crack to peer through. From her hiding place she watched as Madeleine Gauntlet walked back up the stairs in a state of shock with Corny walking behind uttering encouraging remarks.

'That's right, in you get,' Corny said as she climbed back into bed. 'Now close your eyes and think about something nice.'

She lifted her head from the pillow. 'Can

I think about some*body* nice instead?' she asked.

'Certainly,' Corny assured her.

She smiled, lay back down again and closed her eyes.

'In a few minutes you'll have left this dream completely behind,' Cornelius said. 'It will be no more than a distant memory. Sleep will begin to wash all your cares away.'

He began backing out of the bedroom door.

Juliet stepped out of the bathroom and put her finger to her lips. Then the pair of them sneaked downstairs as quietly as they could and let themselves out through the front door.

9

THE NORTHERN MOUNTAINS

On the way back to Bridlington Chawley, Juliet and Cornelius described everything that had happened in Madeleine Gauntlet's house while Otto and Maximillian chuckled appreciatively.

'So what's the next step?' Otto asked when the story was over.

'The fountain in the grounds of Belsham Manor,' Maximillian said. 'Now that we've got Lucas Mendicant's tooth we can make the fountain take us to the right part of Quillipoth. And the sooner we get the clay tablet out of Lucas Mendicant's greedy hands the better. I think we might have to do without sleep altogether and cross over tonight.'

Otto and Juliet groaned. 'We're going to be dead on our feet,' Otto protested.

'Don't worry, I'll give you something to help with that,' Maximillian assured them.

Otto and Juliet looked unconvinced but they were too tired to protest any further. Indeed, by the time they got back to Bridlington Chawley they had both fallen fast asleep, despite the uncomfortable seats in Maximillian's magically-camouflaged car. Cornelius, however, was wide awake. He sat on the parcel shelf at the back, staring out of the car window, his green eyes glinting in the moonlight as he thought about the adventure that lay ahead.

'Come on, you two,' Maximillian said, 'wake up. There's work to be done.'

Otto and Juliet opened their eyes.

'Where are we?' Otto asked, grumpily. His body felt as if it had been crumpled into a ball and stuffed under a wardrobe.

'And what time is it?' Juliet added.

'It's two o'clock in the morning and we're just down the road from Belsham Manor,' Maximillian informed them.

'Oh please, please, please can't we just go home and do this in the morning?' Otto begged.

'You human beings are so limited,' Cornelius said. 'It's the same thing night after night with you – get into bed, close your eyes and fall asleep for the next eight hours. Don't you realise that the night is the best time of all. It's absolutely perfect for hunting!'

'But I don't want to go hunting,' Otto pointed out. 'Besides, it's all right for you, you've been doing nothing but rest since we rescued you from Mr Jones. The rest of us have been rushing around all over the place trying to crack this case.'

Cornelius gave Otto a disparaging look, then turned his back and began washing his leg.

'Don't worry,' Maximillian said. 'I've got just the thing to wake you up.' He reached into his pocket and brought out a paper bag.

'Not sherbet lemons again!' Otto said. 'Look, I'm sorry, Max, but we're going to need a bit more than that if you expect us to go trekking through the mountains of Quillipoth without any sleep.'

'Ah, but these aren't just ordinary sherbet lemons,' Maximillian replied. 'They're enchanted. I took the opportunity to put a fortifying spell on them before you two woke up.'

'What does a fortifying spell do?' Juliet asked suspiciously.

'It gives you extra energy. Take it from me,

once you've eaten one of these you'll feel ready for anything.'

'Hmm! Well I hope they work better than the spell you put on Corny, that's all,' Juliet said, taking the two slightly grubby-looking sweets that Maximillian held out on the palm of his hand and passing one to Otto.

Otto popped the sweet in his mouth. What he would have really liked to do was go back to sleep until the middle of tomorrow morning, then wake up in his own house and have an enormous breakfast of toast, cereal, orange juice, tea, bacon and eggs, and then a bit more toast to round it all off.

Instead he had to make do with one, supposedly enchanted, sherbet lemon, that had little bits of fluff stuck to it suggesting that it had spent rather a lot of time living in Maximillian's coat pocket. He wouldn't be at all surprised to find that there was no such thing as a fortifying spell and that Maximillian had made the whole thing up in the hope of tricking them into imagining they felt better.

'We'll have to leave the car here and go the rest of the way on foot,' Maximillian announced. 'Bring the clothes that you bought in Haverstock and let's keep quiet – in case we bump into Mr Jones' men again.'

They got out of the car and set off for the gates of Belsham Manor, keeping as far as possible to the shadows. As they walked, Otto finally began to wake up properly. He breathed in the night air and stretched. Things weren't too bad really, he decided. He didn't even care if they did bump into Mr Jones, and all his men. In fact he rather hoped they would. It was time there was a showdown.

'I'm sick of all this running away,' he announced suddenly. 'Why don't we take the fight to the enemy. All right – so they're big and muscle-bound, but we can handle them. We can—'

Maximillian clapped a hand over Otto's mouth. 'For goodness sake, keep your voice down, Otto!' he whispered.

'I think he's right,' Juliet said, squaring her shoulders and looking her fiercest, 'Let's stand up for ourselves for a change. After all, we've got magic on our sides.'

Cornelius looked at Maximillian. 'Looks like you made those enchanted sherbet lemons a teeny weeny bit too strong,' he said.

Maximillian sighed. 'Listen, you two,' he said. 'Cornelius is right. It's the sherbet lemons talking. They're making you feel like you could conquer the world right now but you have to try and think straight. We wouldn't stand a chance against Mr Jones and his men. Magic or no magic. They've got guns, remember. All they have to do is pull the trigger whereas I have to conjure up a spell, and that takes time.'

'But they wouldn't kill us,' Otto pointed out. 'That would just be stupid. They need our help, remember.'

'Possibly,' Maximillian said. 'On the other hand Mr Jones might have decided that we know too much and we can't be trusted. If that's the case he won't hesitate to shoot first and ask questions later. So no matter how much you feel like fighting someone, I want you to calm down, keep quiet and follow me. Is that understood?'

He looked at them both very sternly. Reluctantly, they nodded in agreement.

'Good. Now let's try and get to the fountain without any more shouting.'

He led them through the tall iron gates and

into the grounds of Belsham Manor. This time, when they reached the point where the road forked, they took the branch that led to Belsham Manor. The huge old house loomed ahead of them in the moonlight, seeming to float in the darkness like some great ocean liner adrift on a sea of shadows.

After a little while they left the path and cut across the lawn towards a door in the wall at the end of the garden. The garden of Belsham Manor had originally been very much larger. But when the owners had no longer been able to afford to pay enough staff to look after it, they had built a wall to divide the area into two. The smaller part, directly in front of the house, was still kept neat and tidy but the larger part, on the other side of the wall, was simply abandoned. In time it had grown into a wilderness.

It was into this wilderness that Maximillian, Otto, Juliet and Cornelius now passed as they opened the door and stepped through. Immediately they were confronted by a tangle of plants, bushes and trees. It wasn't easy making headway in such a jungle. Branches whipped their faces, unseen roots tripped them up. Only Corny travelled with ease, his keen eyes telling him where to put his paws, his night senses alert to the faintest sounds, smells or noises.

At last they emerged in a clearing where a dried up fountain stood. This area had all been paved and although some plants had grown up in the cracks between the paving stones, there were none of the larger shrubs. It was a perfect place to conduct a magic ritual.

'Right,' Maximillian said. 'If I could have the tooth, Juliet.'

She handed it over.

'Now, you two had better start putting those warm clothes on while I get busy preparing the spell.'

Otto and Juliet put on their anoraks, hats, gloves, scarves and warm socks while Cornelius watched with an ever-so-slightly scornful look in his eye.

'If you had your own fur, you wouldn't need all those additional layers,' he observed.

Meanwhile Maximillian was walking in an anti-clockwise direction around the fountain, chanting quietly to himself. When he had done this he placed the piece of tooth at the base of the fountain, then stepped backwards and made a number of rapid movements with his hands, almost as though he were untying an invisible knot.

'That should do the trick,' he said. Then he, too, put on warm clothes. That done, he ordered Otto to stand on his right hand side with Juliet on his left and Cornelius in front of him, all facing the fountain. He raised both hands high in the air and began to chant:

anna bittee subat irkalla
anna bittee sa eribusu
anna bittee subat alaktasa
anna bittee sa sidibusu

At first nothing much happened. Then slowly a pool of liquid light began to form in the stone basin of the fountain. The pool grew larger and larger until the basin was brimming over and the light began to reach outwards towards them like tentacles of mist. Otto could feel his body buzzing all over, as if an electric current were passing through it. Then, as a finger of light reached out and engulfed him, his whole world turned brilliant white.

A moment later they were no longer in the abandoned garden of Belsham Manor but standing in a clearing on a steep hillside surrounded by enormous, ancient-looking trees. There was snow on the ground and more was falling gently in thick, wet flakes. The air was bitterly cold. Even wrapped in his anorak, scarf and gloves, Otto shivered.

It was hard to say what time it was since the sky above was a uniform grey in colour and there was not even a hint of sun beneath that impenetrable barrier. But Otto had a feeling that it was probably the middle of the morning. This did not surprise him. He had already learnt that time in Quillipoth was not the same as time upon Earth. He looked all around. There was no hint of a path and nothing to see but trees.

Maximillian reached into his pocket and took out a small red flag which he stuck in the ground. 'If we get separated, we meet back here,' he said.

'OK, but which way do we go?' Otto asked.

'Unfortunately I've no idea,' Maximillian replied. 'That's the trouble with magic. It's such an inexact business.'

'That's *one* of the troubles with magic, you mean,' Juliet corrected him. 'I can think of plenty of others.'

'Why don't we follow the music?' Cornelius suggested.

The others looked puzzled. 'What music?' Juliet asked.

Cornelius gave a rather theatrical sigh. 'Honestly, you humans are so badly equipped to survive. I can't imagine how you ever became the dominant species in our world. Just follow me. You'll hear it eventually.' With that, he set off downhill and the others followed.

It wasn't easy going. In places there were hidden springs covered with a thin layer of ice. They could not afford to tread in one of these and get their feet wet. But Cornelius proved a skilful guide and after a while, they all began to hear the 'music' he had referred to earlier. It was anything but tuneful.

'It sounds more like someone smashing up a car,' Otto suggested.

'Or a whole lot of cars,' Juliet added.

The noise grew louder and louder until at last, emerging in a clearing in the forest, they came face to face with its source. An elemental was standing in front of a xylophone-like instrument made of huge metal bars, hitting it furiously with a pair of sturdy-looking hammers. Behind him was a small hut made of branches and thatched with reeds. Against one wall of the hut a large axe was resting beside a pile of firewood. Near the entrance a saucepan hung on a tripod of sticks above a small fire.

Elementals, as Otto and Juliet had discovered on their last trip to Quillipoth, are not as similar to each other in appearance as human beings are. Some have fur on their faces, others have scales, while yet others have skin. They may have horns, tails or even wings.

The elemental responsible for playing the gigantic xylophone (if 'playing' was really the right word to use) had loose greyish skin which hung in folds around his neck, a very long nose like a trunk, and enormous ears. He looked as if he were part elephant and part man.

Around the edge of the clearing were what appeared to be a circle of little stools, though it was hard to say if this was what they really were, for they were so covered with snow that they could easily have been mistaken for a kind of giant white mushroom.

The moment the elemental caught sight of them, he stopped playing, and began walking towards them still carrying his hammer. There was a distinct air of menace about the way he regarded them.

'Good morning!' Maximillian called out, trying to sound as friendly as possible.

'Stay where you are!' the elemental ordered in a loud, booming voice.

It was no surprise to Otto that he could understand what the creature said for, as he had discovered during their last adventure to Quillipoth, the fountain in the grounds of Belsham Manor was woven round with a series of spells, one of which worked as an instantaneous two-way translating service. *Much better than relying on technology*, Otto thought to himself.

'We do not mean you any harm,' he declared.

'Silence!' the elemental roared. He came to a halt a few paces from them. 'Show me your hands!' he told them.

They each held up their hands to show him.

He stared at them for some time in silence. Finally, he said. 'You look like him but you are not him.'

'If I might be allowed to introduce us,' Maximillian said. 'I am Maximillian

Hawksmoor. My friends are Otto Spinoza, Juliet Pennington and Cornelius.'

They each bowed in turn. Otto said, 'We liked your music.'

The elemental's expression changed and for the first time he looked almost friendly. 'One of my own compositions,' he said. 'A great pity you missed the beginning. However, I would be happy to play it again for you, if you so wish.'

'Oh, please don't bother,' Maximillian said quickly. 'We're very grateful for the offer, but we're in a bit of a hurry. Actually, we were wondering if you could tell us how to get to Omustakah.'

'That's easy enough,' the elemental said. 'You have only to follow the path that begins at the other end of this clearing, then keep walking. You will be in Omustakah in a couple of hours.'

'Thanks very much,' Maximillian said.

'Not that it's worth your while visiting the place,' the elemental added.

'Why do you say that?' Otto asked.

The elemental shook his head sadly. 'Since the Ugly One's arrival Omustakah is not what it used to be.'

'The Ugly One?' Otto said. 'Who's he?'

The elemental raised his eyebrows. 'I am surprised that you should ask,' he replied, 'for there is much in common between his features and yours. Indeed, I thought at first that he might be among you for it is said that he often goes about in disguise.'

'So you're saying that we're ugly, too?' Juliet said.

'You are certainly far from beautiful,' the elemental replied, 'but that is not your fault so let us say no more about it.'

'That's very generous of you.'

The elemental nodded as if he thought it was indeed, a generous thing to say.

'I can assure you, we are who we say we are,' Maximillian told him.

'I believe you,' the elemental replied, 'for it is well known that however much he changes his appearance, the Ugly One can always be told by a ring with a green stone upon it that he cannot conceal. That is why I asked to see your hands. Now perhaps you would like to take some tea with me?'

'We really have to go...' Maximillian began.

'You refuse my hospitality?' the elemental snarled menacingly.

'We'd love some tea,' Otto declared, 'wouldn't we?'

'Can't think of anything nicer,' Juliet agreed.

The elemental led the way to his hut. Inside, there was just one room with a mattress and a few blankets. On one wall there was a rough shelf on which a few simple cooking utensils were ranged. From this shelf, the elemental took down four mugs. Into these he poured a black foul-smelling liquid from the pot above the fire. Otto pretended to sip his, then he put it down on the floor beside him.

The elemental sat down facing them, his legs crossed. 'My name is Nork,' he began. 'Once I was the Kabolim's Master of Music and one of his most trusted advisers, though you would not think so to look at me now.'

'What happened?' Juliet asked.

'Was it the arrival of the Ugly One?' Otto asked.

'Exactly. From the day he entered the city he began pouring his poison into the Kabolim's ear. I tried to do my duty and warn the Kabolim that he should not listen. And what was my reward? I was banished to this forest. Everything I owned was taken from me and given to the Ugly One, except for my musical instrument which for some reason he did not want.'

'I wonder why that was?' Otto said.

'Who can say? But I will have my revenge one day,' Nork replied. He suddenly sprang to his feet. 'Let me show you something.'

They all got up again and followed him out of the hut. He walked over to the ring of snow-covered stumps that Otto had assumed were stools and brushed the snow from one of them – to reveal a severed head stuck on a wooden spike. Though it was somewhat shrivelled it was clearly the head of an elemental. There were two small horns on the top, the ears were pointed and the nose was very broad but otherwise it was quite human-looking. The eyes were still wide open and as Otto stared at them in horror they seemed to look back at him with an expression of pain and terror.

Nork moved on to the next stump and brushed off the snow to reveal another head. This one was striped like a zebra. Its mouth was open in an expression of agony. Nork considered it for a moment then smiled as if in satisfaction before moving on once more.

When he had uncovered the whole grisly circle he turned back to his guests. 'These were my enemies,' he said. 'Each one of them I slew with my own hand. There are ninety-nine in all. But as you see, there is one stake yet uncrowned.'

They looked in the direction that he pointed and saw that it was true.

'That is where I shall place the Ugly One's head, when my time comes,' Nork told them.

'Right,' Maximillian said, trying to hide his alarm. 'Well, I must say I've enjoyed our little chat but I really think we ought to be on our way.'

'But you have not finished your tea,' Nork objected.

'We're not really big tea drinkers,' Otto told him. 'In fact, we're trying to give it up altogether.'

'We're very glad to have met you though,' Juliet told him.

All four of them began backing away.

Nork watched them go. He knew that he had frightened them and he was glad. 'You will be back, my friends,' he said to himself, 'and you will bring the Ugly One with you. I can feel it in my bones.'

He picked up the axe that rested against the wall of his hut. A crooked smile spread slowly across his face. 'And when you come, I will be waiting,' he added, gently testing the blade with his finger.

10

THE UGLY ONE

After they had been walking for about half an hour the trees began to thin out. Soon Otto and his friends emerged on a steep hillside, looking down into a deep valley. Below them the city of Omustakah sprawled untidily, as though it had been flung there carelessly by some giant hand.

'Another hour or so should do it,' Maximillian said, optimistically. 'Come on, at least it might be marginally warmer down there.'

When they finally reached the outskirts of Omustakah they found a busy, bustling city, where the cold weather was no obstacle to everyday life.

Horse drawn carriages piled high with goods of every kind rattled along the cobbled streets. Shops displayed piles of animal skins and furs, and elementals haggled with each other over prices.

Just like in Abirkadash, which they had visited the previous summer, there were plenty of stores selling steaming heaps of animal intestines, or Paunchy Pudding as it was known, the elemental's favourite delicacy. There were also lots of cafés in which dull-eyed elementals sat smoking long pipes of ziff, the drug that they believed increased their magical powers, but that also made them extremely unpredictable.

But there the similarity ended. The streets of Abirkadash had been a riot of colour, its inhabitants clothed in every fashion imaginable. Omustakah, on the other hand, was a drab-looking place, like a picture that someone had sketched in charcoal. The houses all seemed to have been built of the same grey stone and the city's inhabitants all dressed alike, the males in tall black hats and thick black fur-lined cloaks, the females in brown cloth hats that covered their ears, and matching brown cloaks.

At every street corner Otto and his friends passed groups of elementals huddled together, warming their hands at charcoal braziers and drinking cups of the same stinking, black tea that Nork had offered them. The tea-drinkers glanced suspiciously at the newcomers, sometimes spitting on the ground as they passed.

'Ever had the feeling that you're not welcome?' Otto said.

'Do you think it's because we look like the Ugly One?' Juliet suggested.

'Probably,' Otto replied, 'but I get the feeling there might be more to it than that. No one looks very cheerful. Have you noticed that?'

'Perhaps it's the cold,' Juliet suggested. 'I'm not sure I'd be cheerful if I had to put up with weather like this.'

Otto shook his head. 'Something tells me it's not just the weather,' he said.

They had come to a great crossroads. Wide boulevards led off in four directions and down one of them, dozens of elementals were streaming purposefully, like a crowd heading for a football match. 'There seems to be something important going on down there,' Maximillian said. 'Perhaps we ought to go and take a look.'

They followed the crowd down the street. Many of the elementals glanced in their direction and their expressions were far from friendly.

'Are you sure we should be doing this?' Otto asked.

'We have to find out what's going on,' Maximillian replied. 'Information is the detective's primary tool, remember.'

At last the crowd turned into a narrow side street where they soon found themselves packed together as thickly as travellers on the London Underground at rush-hour. Everyone was forced to slow their pace to a crawl. Yet, despite the crush, the elementals all seemed to keep their distance from Otto, Juliet Maximillian and Cornelius, as if no one wanted to appear to be connected with them.

At last they reached the end of the side street where the crowd spilled out into an open square, lined on every side with tall buildings. The place was already packed with elementals of every kind and a great hubbub of conversation rose from the crowd like the buzzing of angry bees.

At one end of the square a primitive wooden stage had been erected and a huge elemental with a single horn in the middle of his head, like a rhinoceros, got up to address the crowd.

'My fellow citizens,' he began, his powerful

voice easily carrying to all sections of the crowd. Immediately all conversation ceased and every eye was turned in his direction.

'You all know why this meeting has been called,' he continued. 'Once upon a time Omustakah was a city we were proud to live in, a city that was famous for its power and its might. Not any more. Once upon a time we had a ruler whose name was feared throughout the world. Not any more. Once upon a time our enemies, the Nevatski horsemen, did not dare to show their filthy faces in our town. Not any more. Now they raid and loot our city at will. And why is this? Why have we become a laughing stock in the eyes of the world and easy prey for our enemies? I will tell you why. It is because the Kabolim has grown weak!'

The audience roared their approval.

'And we all know when this change began,' the rhino-headed elemental continued. 'The very day that the Ugly One appeared in our city.'

'Death to the Ugly One!' someone shouted. Immediately the cry was taken up by the rest of the crowd.

While the crowd was busy working itself into

a frenzy, another elemental clambered up onto the stage and whispered something in the ear of the rhino-headed elemental. He nodded, then raised his hand for silence.

'I have just been informed of a most grave development,' he announced when the chanting had finally died down. 'It seems that three more of the Ugly One's kind have appeared in our city. Not only that but they have had the audacity to come here to this very square in order to spy upon our meeting.'

All around Otto, Juliet and Maximillian heads began turning in their direction. 'Here they are!' someone shouted.

'Seize them!' someone else called.

Otto turned round frantically looking for an escape route, but there was nowhere to run. Rough hands took hold of him. Others seized Juliet and Maximillian.

'Run, Corny!' Juliet shouted. And he did, slipping deftly through the legs of the crowd without anyone noticing.

Meanwhile Otto, Maximillian and Juliet were dragged to the front of the square and up onto the stage as elementals jeered and spat in their direction.

'Do we want three more Ugly Ones to make a mockery of our city?' the rhino-headed elemental demanded.

'No!' the crowd roared back.

It was no good Otto, Juliet or Maximillian protesting that they were nothing to do with the Ugly One, that they had no intention of making a mockery of the city, or that they meant no harm whatsoever. Nobody was in the mood for listening, least of all the rhino-headed elemental.

'What do we do with enemies of Omustakah?' he bellowed.

Immediately the cry came back, louder than ever: 'Cut off their heads!'

The rhino-headed elemental nodded to one of his cronies and from somewhere a great block of wood was dragged onto the stage.

Fear coursed through Otto's body like cold fire. He glanced desperately at Maximillian who was struggling to get his hands free from the clutches of two snake-skinned elementals. As Otto watched, Maximillian kicked one of his captors on the shin with his heel and for a moment the snake-skinned elemental loosened his grip. It was enough for

171

Maximillian to get one arm free. Frantically, he began making a series of passes in the air while at the same time chanting.

'He's going to get us out of here!' Otto thought, his heart soaring with hope.

But a moment later the snake-skinned elemental recovered himself and brought the side of his hand down on Maximillian's neck in a fierce chopping movement. Maximillian slumped forward lifelessly. Their last hope was gone.

'You first!' the rhino-headed elemental said, pointing at Otto.

Otto's captors, two unusually tall elementals with fur on their faces and small pointed ears, dragged him over to the wooden block. He fought against them with all his strength but his legs were kicked from beneath him and a moment later he was kneeling in front of the block. Beside him stood the rhino-headed elemental, now clutching an axe. 'Put your head on the block!' he ordered.

Otto tried to push himself away from the block but another elemental stepped forward and grabbed his hair, yanking his head forward.

I'm going to die! Otto thought as his head was

pulled down fiercely onto the wooden block. He was so terrified that he could no longer hear the roaring of the crowd. Instead, he withdrew deep into his mind and everything grew terribly still. He wondered if it would hurt very much to have his head cut off.

He thought about his mother sitting on the sofa in the flat above the shop where he had left her. Now no one would come to awaken her from her enchanted sleep. What would become of her? He had not even said goodbye. He felt tears springing to his eyes.

What happened next made no sense to him. The hands that were gripping his arms and his hair suddenly released him. *Was that it?* he wondered. Was he already dead? But there had been no impact, no pain, no sense of the world slipping away from him.

He lifted his head and immediately the noise of the crowd came rushing back as though he had emerged from under water. He was not dead after all, he discovered, but the elementals who had been holding him certainly were. They lay on the stage with arrows sticking out of their throats and blood dripping from their wounds. Even as he took in this astonishing news, he heard a whoosh and another arrow lodged in the chest of the rhino-headed elemental who staggered backwards and collapsed.

Otto could see arrows raining down on the crowd without a break. Elementals rushed about frantically in all directions, knocking each other over as they struggled to get out of the square. Otto looked all round trying to discover where the arrows were coming from. Then he saw them – rows of archers clothed in red tunics standing on the rooftops firing volley after volley into the square.

Otto turned back to the stage to see Juliet standing opposite him, her eyes wide in amazement. She too had been released from her captors' grasp. Between them Maximillian was getting groggily to his feet, holding his head in one hand. 'What's happening?' he asked. But neither Otto nor Juliet were able to enlighten him.

Now a scarlet tide began to flood into the square as more troops poured in from every side. In some places there was hand-to-hand fighting. In other places elementals surrendered without a fight and lay face-down on the ground with their hands above their heads.

A man – not an elemental but a man – was making his way through the crowd towards the stage, flanked on either side by a bodyguard of burly-looking elementals carrying swords and shields. There was something very odd about the way he was dressed. Otto couldn't think at first what it was. Then he realised that the man was wearing a suit and tie – with a red cloak thrown over his shoulders. Within moments he was climbing onto the stage beside them.

'Allow me to introduce myself,' he said. 'I am Lucas Mendicant. I believe you've been looking for me.'

They stared back at him, unable to think of a single word to say in reply.

This seemed to amuse him. 'Don't tell me you've come all this way and now you're tongue-tied?' he said. 'Well, never mind. I'm sure we'll have lots to say to each other back at the palace. Come on.'

They had no choice but to follow. A phalanx of guards lined up on either side of them, hurrying them off the stage. Juliet looked round frantically for Cornelius but there was no sign of him. Soon they had made their way through the square where the fighting was already almost over and were being ushered into a waiting carriage which took off with an escort of mounted soldiers both in front and behind.

'That was a close thing,' Otto said when he had finally recovered sufficiently from his surprise to speak. 'I thought it was all over back there.'

'Don't speak too soon,' Maximillian told him. 'We may only have leapt from the frying pan into the fire.'

'I don't care,' Otto said. 'At least I've still got my head on my shoulders.'

'But what about Corny?' Juliet said. 'I hope he's all right.'

'That cat can look after himself,' Maximillian observed. 'We're the ones who could be in trouble.'

The building before which their carriage eventually drew up was built on a colossal scale and crowned with three huge golden domes, the first brightly-coloured things that they had seen since their arrival in Omustakah. As they got out and stood looking upwards, Lucas Mendicant disembarked from another coach and marched over to join them. 'Quite a sight, isn't it?' he said. 'Still we mustn't stand here talking. Come along, chop-chop. We've got things to do you know.'

He sounded so bright and breezy and so completely reasonable, Otto had difficulty remembering that this man was not to be trusted. He had swindled Haverstock University out of three million pounds and stolen a rare and immensely dangerous object from the British Museum.

They followed him into the palace, still escorted on either side by a phalanx of elementals in red tunics. As they went, Lucas Mendicant gave them a running commentary.

'This is the Grand Entrance Hall. The original was much smaller and less impressive. The Kabolim had it entirely redesigned to celebrate the battle of Navgodirod when he personally slaughtered one hundred and fifty Nevatski horsemen. The chandeliers are made from a kind of rock crystal that is so difficult to mine, they say fifty elementals die underground for every cubic metre of it that is produced. And this is known as the Purple Room for obvious reasons. As you can see, every single item of furniture or decoration is purple. I'm afraid

I find it rather disgusting but it's one of the Kabolim's favourite rooms, so not a word of criticism if you please.' He continued in this vein as they made their way through one lavishly-furnished room after another, at last arriving at a small chamber towards the back of the palace.

'You can wait outside,' he told the soldiers, ushering Otto and his friends through the doorway.

Unlike every other room they had visited, this one was plainly furnished with a large oak desk, a couple of leather armchairs, some straight-backed wooden chairs, a filing cabinet and an awful lot of bookshelves. There was something about the room that looked extremely familiar. Suddenly Otto realised where he had seen it before.

'It's like the furniture in the University of Haverstock,' he said.

Lucas Mendicant smiled. 'But of course it is. That's exactly where it came from. I had everything in my office transported here by magic. Makes me feel much more at home. Now then, that's enough small talk. Let's get down to business. Sit down, all of you.'

They did as they were told, Maximillian in one of the armchairs, Otto and Juliet on a couple of straight-backed chairs. Lucas Mendicant sat at his desk and leant back with his arms folded, looking enormously pleased with himself. 'First of all, I should tell you that I know exactly why you're here,' he began. 'You're after the clay tablet that I took from the museum. Well, I can assure you, you're not going to get it. See this ring?'

He held up his right hand. On the index finger was a gold ring with a large green stone set in its centre. 'It was given to me by the Kabolim in gratitude for my services to him. I have no idea where he got it from and neither does he. He probably took it off someone he killed and then forgot all about it. It doesn't matter. The point is that it has all sorts of magical powers, such as enabling me to come and go between worlds whenever I wish. Of course it's nothing like as powerful as the clay tablet. Not in the same league. But still quite powerful enough for me to prevent you from trying any little magic tricks against me. A moment's thought and I can cancel out your most powerful spells. So if you had any ideas about overpowering me, it's advisable to forget all about them. Understood?' He looked at them all, waiting for a reply.

'Understood,' Maximillian told him.

'Good. Now then I'll start by explaining a few things. As you can see, I'm pretty much in charge of this place.'

'What's happened to the Kabolim?' asked Maximillian. 'I suppose you've killed him.'

Lucas Mendicant laughed. 'Killed him! Of course not. He's far too useful for me to kill him.'

'Then where is he?'

'Playing golf,' Lucas Mendicant said. 'In fact if you look out of that window you should be able to spot him.'

Otto, Juliet and Maximillian all got up and went over to the window Lucas Mendicant had indicated. Sure enough in the distance they could see an enormous elemental with an upper body like a bull's swinging a golf club as if he was hoping to knock the ball into orbit.

'I introduced him to the game,' Lucas Mendicant went on. 'I thought it might be a useful way of diverting his attention from my own plans. It always used to work with the

Dean of Haverstock. He wasn't sure about it at first but now it's a complete obsession for him. He doesn't think about anything else.'

'That's why the elementals were complaining about him,' Juliet said.

'Don't talk to me about elementals,' Lucas Mendicant said. 'I'm sick to death of them. You've no idea what it's been like living here for the last few months. The food is absolutely atrocious.'

'Is that why you stole all those cartons of breakfast cereal?' Otto asked.

'Oh, you know about those, do you?' Lucas Mendicant said. 'Well, what else could I do? Do you know what they have for breakfast here? Raw gizzard of mountain sheep in a bowl of warm blood.'

'What about the paracetamol?' Juliet asked.

'My word, you have been doing your homework!' Lucas Mendicant said. 'Since you ask, I got them for the Kabolim. He used to get the most terrible headaches. For some reason even the most powerful magic couldn't cure them. I happened to have a couple of painkillers in my pocket when I first arrived which was a pretty big stroke of luck as it happened because elementals were on the point of killing me when I saw that the Kabolim was holding his head and making the most dreadful grimaces – so I said I had something that might help him out. Now I'm his favourite person. He's chopped the heads off all his ministers and put me in charge of the government. And I'll tell you something else: he's a completely different person since he started taking the tablets. Lost all his interest in war. Still quite violent of course but in a jolly sort of way. Nowadays he only chops the heads off anyone who is foolish enough to beat him at golf.'

'So if you've got him eating out of your hand as you say you have, why do you need the clay tablet?' Maximillian asked.

Lucas Mendicant sighed. 'Because I want to go home,' he said. 'I'm sick to death of this place.'

'You can go home any time you choose,' Juliet pointed out.

'Ah yes, but I can't stay there, can I?' Lucas Mendicant replied. 'There's a small matter of three million pounds, which I owe to the University of Haverstock. Besides, when I go back to our world it's got to be on my terms.'

'And what are they?' Maximillian asked.

'Oh, that's easy!' said another voice.

Otto, Juliet and Maximillian turned their heads. Madame Sikursky was standing behind them. 'Lucas and I are going to be in charge – of everything. We're going to rule the world. And you, my friends, are going to make it possible.'

11

THE SMALL PRINT

'Ah, Marushka,' Lucas Mendicant said. 'So glad you could join us. As you see our friends are all here. The young lady who burgled your hotel room, the young man with the very interesting ancestry, and the magical detective.' He smiled at Maximillian. 'Oh yes, we know all about you too, Mr Hawksmoor. We've also done our research. But of course it's Otto we're really interested in.'

'That's right,' Madame Sikursky said, sitting down in the empty armchair. 'You see we've been searching for the Forbidden Spell for some time. Lucas was getting close and then he had to leave our own world and come here. So when I heard about the clay tablet I got in touch with him and he removed it from the British Museum for safekeeping.'

'Safekeeping!' Otto said, scornfully. 'You mean he stole it.'

'We couldn't have just anybody looking at it,' Lucas Mendicant said. 'The Forbidden Spell is far too powerful a weapon for that. It needs to be wielded by an individual of discipline, strength of mind, and supreme intelligence.'

'By which you mean yourself, I suppose?' Maximillian said.

'Naturally. The knowledge on this clay tablet has to be handled properly. We can't afford to make any mistakes.'

'The Babylonians blew themselves up,' Maximillian pointed out, 'and so will you.'

Lucas Mendicant shook his head. 'That's just where you're wrong. We will control the power of the tablet. But enough of this time wasting. Otto, we require your cooperation.'

Otto shook his head. 'No chance!' he said.

Lucas Mendicant held up the index finger of his right hand. The magic ring glinted with an inner light. 'On the contrary,' he said. 'You will do exactly as you are told and your companions will be powerless to assist you. Now stand up, Otto!'

Juliet and Maximillian watched in dismay as Otto got to his feet.

Mendicant nodded. 'He's all yours Marushka.'

Madame Sikursky got up from her chair and stood directly in front of Otto, fixing her huge black eyes on his. 'Now, Otto, I am going to take you back through all the years of your life,' she told him, 'back to a time before you were even born. Let your breathing slow down. Feel yourself beginning to relax.'

Despite his efforts to resist, Otto almost immediately found his body growing loose and his eyes closing. Within moments he was travelling along the now familiar tunnel of light. The years flashed by, one after the other and the great tumult of the centuries washed over him.

'When I say the word *stop*, you will have arrived on the very last day of the Tower of Babel, Otto.' Madame Sikursky continued. 'You will find yourself witnessing the moments before the great explosion. You will listen, you will observe and you will report everything back to me. Stop!'

The tunnel of light contracted around Otto, and a moment later he was standing in the stone tower watching his ancestor, Balshazzar, in conversation with his chief magician. The

Chief Magician was pointing to a set of symbols inscribed on a clay tablet.

'With these symbols a magician can unlock the energy that lies at the very heart of the universe,' he explained, 'he can destroy the world in the blink of an eye.'

'Tell me what they are saying, Otto!' Madame Sikursky's eager voice broke in.

Otto had no choice but to repeat the words he had just overheard. And as the Chief Magician continued, explaining exactly how the symbols should be visualised in the mind, Otto relayed every detail back to Madame Sikursky.

Only when the conversation between Balshazzar and his Chief Magician was at an end and Otto had repeated every scrap of knowledge, did Madame Sikursky release him from her hypnotic spell. A moment later he was standing in Lucas Mendicant's office once more. Ashamed of what he had just been made to do, he covered his face with his hands.

Maximillian stood up and put his arm around him. 'It's all right, Otto,' he said. 'There wasn't anything else you could have done.'

'How touching!' Lucas Mendicant mocked as

he, too, got to his feet. 'And how true! Soon everyone on Earth will be in the same position as you, Otto. They will have no choice but to do as I tell them. For I shall have the power to unmake the world!'

'Come on, Lucas,' Madame Sikursky interrupted. 'We've got all the information we need. Use your ring to take us back to Earth and let's get started on the real work.'

Lucas Mendicant gave her a long look then shook his head slowly. 'I'm sorry Marushka,' he said, 'I'm afraid you're not going anywhere.'

Madame Sikursky's face fell. 'What are you talking about?' she demanded.

Lucas Mendicant raised one eyebrow. 'You didn't really imagine I was going to share my power with you, did you?' he said. 'There's only room for one ruler of the world and that makes you surplus to requirements.'

Madame Sikursky snatched the tablet from the table. 'You won't do much conquering without this,' she cried.

But Lucas Mendicant merely pointed to the tablet with his ring finger and it vanished from her hand, reappearing simultaneously in his own. Then he muttered some words under his breath, there was a sound like a soft explosion and where Madame Sikursky had stood a moment earlier there was now just a little pile of dust.

For a moment Lucas Mendicant looked almost stunned by what he had done and seemed to forget that there was anyone else in the room. Perhaps he wasn't entirely without feeling.

Whatever the case, this was Otto's opportunity. But could he take it?

A situation like this calls for hunchability, he said to himself.

He forced himself to stop thinking about what had just happened. Instead he let his mind go completely blank. And suddenly he knew exactly what to do.

When Balshazzar's Chief Magician had explained how the Forbidden Spell worked, he had been concentrating on the three large rows of symbols at the top of the clay tablet. There was, however, another smaller symbol at the bottom of the tablet which he had not mentioned. Otto had no idea what this lesser symbol was for but he had the strongest feeling that it could help him, as if the Chief Magician had included it on the tablet in case it was needed in some sort of emergency.

He closed his eyes and tried to visualise the symbol. Almost immediately it sprang to life before his mind's eye, as if it had always been there waiting for him to look at it. The more he concentrated, the brighter the symbol grew until it was glowing like a firework in the night.

When the Chief Magician had instructed Balshazzar about using the symbols he had said, 'You must make the symbols vibrate in your mind, like a bell that is struck in an empty room. You must concentrate on those vibrations, making them grow and grow until they fill the whole world.'

Otto let the image of the symbol roll over him like a wave, washing away everything but itself. There was only the symbol vibrating inside his head, glowing brighter and brighter with every moment.

Suddenly the symbol began to spin. Faster and faster it turned until there was an explosion of light and Otto felt the world give an almighty pop, as though a cork the size of a planet had been pulled out of a bottle the size of a galaxy.

When he recovered he found that he was

standing in what looked like a large and rather dusty old attic. Three elderly women were gazing at him with an air of amused surprise. From the resemblance in their faces it was clear that they were sisters.

'Well, what do we have here?' asked the first sister. Dressed in a deep red, floor-length gown she was tall and thin with wild curly hair and twinkly eyes. She was clearly the youngest of the three.

'A visitor!' exclaimed the second sister. Dressed in green, she was short and dumpy with her grey hair arranged in an orderly bun. 'My goodness,' she went on, 'we haven't had a visitor for, let me see, well it must be at least...'

'Four thousand years, six months and seven days exactly,' said the third and oldest sister. Her gown was midnight blue, She had a stern face with high cheekbones and rather cold blue eyes from which she regarded Otto as though he were an unexpected specimen of insect-life she had accidentally come across. 'We're very busy here you know,' she told him. 'Kindly state your name and purpose.'

'My name is Otto Spinoza,' he replied. 'I'm afraid I don't really know what my purpose is.

You see I got here by concentrating on a symbol from the Forbidden Spell, even though I didn't really know what it would do. I have to stop Lucas Mendicant from taking over the world and I also need to rescue Juliet and Maximillian who are trapped in Omustakah and I don't even know what's happened to Corny but I think he got lost when the elementals were going to chop off our heads and—'

'Whoah!' said the youngest sister. 'Let's go a little bit more slowly, shall we?'

'Sorry,' Otto said.

'No problem. Now just take a deep breath and start all over again.'

Otto hesitated, but something told him he could trust these women. So he started again from the beginning. He told them about being a magical detective, about being kidnapped by Mr Jones' men, about the theft of the clay tablet, about the way Madame Sikursky had forced him to reveal its secrets, and about his idea to see what the smaller symbol at the bottom of the tablet had meant.

'And I'm sorry if this sounds rude,' he concluded, 'but I have no idea who you are or even *where* you are but if there is some way you can possibly help me, I'd be extremely grateful.'

The oldest sister looked disapproving. 'They all say they're going to be grateful. Fat lot of good it ever does us.'

'Now, now, Lachesis,' said the middle sister, 'you can't hold poor Otto responsible for what other people may or may not have done.' She turned back to Otto. 'As for who we are, you are talking to the Fates, young man, the ultimate controllers of human destiny. I am Atropos. And these are my sisters Lachesis and Clothos.'

The Fates! Otto recalled the conversation he had had with Maximillian about coincidence. 'In the olden days magicians used to believe that there were these three goddesses called The Fates,' Maximillian had said. 'But we modern magicians don't believe in stuff like that any more.' So much for modern magicians!

'As to whether or not we can help you,' Atropos continued, 'I'm afraid it all depends on the regulations.'

The youngest sister got to her feet. 'We will have to consult the book,' she said. For the first time Otto noticed that the walls of the room were lined with hundreds and hundreds of enormous leather-bound volumes. One of these, the youngest sister now took down from a shelf, staggering a little under its weight. Then she blew off the cobwebs and deposited the book on a table in the middle of the room with a hefty thump. She put on a pair of glasses that had been hanging on a chain around her neck, opened the book and began leafing through its pages muttering to herself, 'Otto Spindle, Otto Spinneker, Otto Spinnet, Otto Spinfoil. Ah yes, here you are, Otto Spinoza.'

'I'm in your book?' Otto said in astonishment.

Clothos regarded him over the top of her glasses. 'My dear boy,' she said, 'Everyone is in our book.' She turned back to the book and began reading. Soon a frown creased her brow. 'My word!' she said. 'You have got yourself into a right pickle, haven't you?' She closed the book. 'Unfortunately, there's not a lot that can be done about it. You see there's only a certain amount of bending of the rules that can be done on any particular day and what with all this travelling between worlds, you've pretty much used up your allowance. No, I'm afraid the only thing that can still be changed is the Kabolim's golf match and only the very last ball of that.'

Otto looked at her in dismay. 'The Kabolim's golf match! But that's no use to me.'

'I'm sorry,' Clothos said, sounding rather put out at Otto's response. 'It's the best that we can do.' She sat down again.

'You see,' Lachesis told her. 'They all start out promising they're going to be eternally grateful. Then when you try to help out, this is what you get.'

'I'm sorry,' Otto said. 'I didn't mean to sound ungrateful. It's just that...'

But it was too late. Everything in the room began spinning round like water draining out of a sink. Otto found himself caught up in the flow and sucked into a well of nothingness. A moment later he was back in Lucas Mendicant's office.

'Well I'll say goodbye then,' Lucas Mendicant was saying. 'I hate to leave you here all by yourselves but you shouldn't be short of company for very long. According to my spies, there's a group of Nevatski horsemen heading for the palace even as we speak. They should be here in about five minutes. Do give them my regards. Oh and by the way...'

But that was as far as he got because at that precise moment there was a crash of broken glass and a golf ball hurtled through the window and struck him on the head. For a second he looked utterly astonished. Then his eyelids closed and he fell to the ground.

12

TRANSMOGRIFICATION

'He's dead,' Maximillian said, bending over Lucas Mendicant and feeling for his pulse.

'That was a bit of luck,' Juliet said.

'Luck had absolutely nothing to do with it,' Otto told her. 'I'll explain all about it later. But right now, I think we'd better get out of here as quickly as possible before the Nevatski horsemen, the citizens of Omustakah or the Kabolim himself catches up with us.'

'First things first,' Maximillian said. He slid the ring off Lucas Mendicant's finger and placed it on his own. Then he got to his feet, picked up the clay tablet and put it in his pocket. 'Right,' he said. 'Now we're ready.'

Otto opened the door, and peered out into the corridor. There was no sign of any guards. 'Perhaps someone's tipped them off about what's coming,' he suggested.

197

They stepped out into the corridor and made their way cautiously through the palace, retracing the route by which they had originally been brought to Lucas Mendicant's office. Not once did they see a guard or even a servant. The palace was as deserted as the deck of the *Marie Celeste*.

At last they arrived at the Grand Entrance Hall. The two great wooden doors were closed. Maximillian opened one of them just a crack and peered at the outside world. Immediately an arrow thudded into the door above his head and stuck there, quivering. He quickly ducked back inside again and shut the door.

'Looks like we'll have to find another way out,' he said. But even as he spoke these words they heard shouts coming from the rear of the building.

'They must be inside!' Juliet said. 'We can't go back that way.'

'We'll have to go up!' Maximillian said.

'Not this again!' Otto said to himself, remembering the last time they had found themselves trapped inside a palace in Quillipoth. But there was no time for discussion. They raced up the grand staircase, taking the steps two at a time. As they reached the first landing, Otto caught sight of armed elementals bursting into the Grand Entrance Hall.

'They're right behind us!' he yelled.

A moment later, another arrow sailed past his head and lodged in a wooden statue of the Kabolim.

'Faster!' Maximillian urged them.

They kept going up. No one stopped to think whether this was a good idea or what they would do when they reached the top floor. By the time he had climbed eight flights of stairs, Otto's legs had turned to jelly and he was suffering from a nagging stitch in his side. The good news was that there were no more stairs left to climb. The bad news was that the Nevatski horsemen were still on their tail.

'What do we do now?' he asked.

Maximillian hesitated. 'That way,' he decided, pointing down a long wood-panelled corridor.

'Why?' Otto asked.

Maximillian shrugged. 'Hunchability,' he said. 'Come on!'

They ran along the corridor past a series of

closed doors, trying each one in turn only to find them all locked. At the furthest end, however, a door stood open, revealing a lavish bedroom dominated by a huge four-poster bed.

'In there!' Maximillian ordered.

They followed him inside and shut the door behind them, locking it with the key that, fortunately, was still in the lock.

'That won't hold them for long,' Otto said. He glanced around the room and lighted on a chest of drawers. 'We could push that against the door,' he suggested. The others agreed and together they shoved it across the floor, wedging it beneath the handle of the door.

'What are we going to do now?' Juliet asked.

'We're going to find a way out,' Maximillian said, sounding remarkably calm considering their situation. He crossed the room to the window and drew back the curtains. French windows gave onto a small balcony with an iron railing running all round it. 'What a splendid view!' he said. He stood staring out at the city of Omustakah that lay stretched before them like an illustration from a child's picture book.

'I don't want to interrupt any great thoughts

you might be having,' Juliet said after a while, 'but I think I can smell burning.'

'Oh, great!' Otto said. 'They're not even going to bother breaking the door down, they're just going to burn us alive.'

Still Maximillian remained motionless.

'Max!' Juliet said. 'Snap out of it! We have to get out of here somehow.'

Maximillian blinked and gazed at her with a confused expression. Then he gave a deep sigh. 'You're quite right,' he said. 'Don't worry, I have a plan.'

'What does it involve?' Otto asked, glancing towards the doorway where smoke was beginning to curl upwards from the space between the door and the floor.

'Transmogrification,' Maximillian said.

'Trans what?'

'Transmogrification,' Maximillian replied. 'It's like the spell I used on Cornelius only more elaborate. In Corny's case I merely shifted his real self to an in between world while creating a brooch to act as a vehicle that could be used to return him to our own world at a later date.'

'And in this case?' Otto asked.

'In this case I am going to transform

our bodies at a genetic level.'

'You say this is more difficult than the spell you used on Cornelius?' Juliet said.

'That's right.'

'But that one didn't work properly.'

'I know,' Maximillian said, 'but I'll get it right this time. I promise.' He opened the French windows. 'Now I need you to stand on the balcony.'

Otto and Juliet looked at each other, shrugged in desperation and stepped out through the French windows.

'I hope he's not going to suggest jumping,' Otto said.

'I need complete silence for a little while, if you don't mind,' Maximillian told them. 'I'm going to have to use the power of Lucas Mendicant's ring and I haven't really got much idea how it works. It's elemental magic, you see and that's completely different to human magic.'

Otto and Juliet stood rather nervously on the balcony, trying to resist the temptation to look down. It was cold out there and a few flakes of snow were beginning to drift gently downwards. One settled on Otto's nose and melted. He wiped it away.

Why do I keep getting involved in all this? he asked himself. At that precise moment he could not think of a good answer.

For about five minutes Maximillian simply stood there with his head in his hands, looking as if he were in severe pain. All the time the room behind him was gradually filling up with smoke.

At last he gave another deep sigh and looked up. 'All right, I think I can do it,' he told them, 'but I have to warn you, it's going to hurt quite a lot. I tried to think of a way round the pain but I couldn't. Do you still want to go ahead with it?'

'If it's either that or burn to death, then I think I'll settle for the trans-whatever-you-call-it,' Otto said.

Juliet nodded. 'Me, too.'

'Right then, here we go.' Maximillian stepped onto the balcony beside them and closed the windows behind him. It was a little crowded now that there were three of them. Max raised his arms at either side and began to chant. At least, chanting was the only word that Otto could think of for the sound that came out of

Maximillian's mouth. Really it was more like a mixture of human and animal noises. There were grunts and snorts and howls and several times Maximillian whistled a note so sharp and piercing that it made Otto's ears hurt.

It was after the last of these whistles that Otto began to feel the spell working. It started with the most appalling pain that made him double up and clutch at his stomach, retching as if he were about to be violently sick. At the same time his arms and his legs grew tighter and tighter, as if the skin was shrinking, and the top of his head seemed to be on fire. He wanted to scream but he had no control over his mouth. It felt as though someone were kneading his face like dough.

He had never known such pain in his life before. The spell must have gone wrong, he decided. Whatever Maximillian had intended, it can't have been this. This was worse than being burnt to death. It was like being stamped to death by someone with spiked shoes. It was like being torn into a thousand little pieces with each little piece still alive and in agony. It was like the worst torture that anyone could ever imagine. It was like…

And then suddenly it was over and everything was different. He was still on the balcony but much lower down than he had been before. He couldn't understand why that was. Had he collapsed? Was he lying in a heap on the ground? He simply couldn't tell. All he knew was that something very strange had happened to his body.

For the first time since the pain had hit him, he thought about Maximillian and Juliet. Had the spell worked for them? He tried to look at them but his eyesight didn't seem to be working properly. Instead of just moving his eyeballs, he was forced to turn his whole head to look around. And when he did, he finally understood.

Beside him on the balcony perched two large, black birds. One of them wore a small silver band around one leg in the centre of which was a large green stone.

He turned his head once more, trying to see his own body. He stretched out one of his arms and examined it. It wasn't an arm any more. It was a feathered wing. He opened his mouth – no, he opened his beak – and tried to speak. All that came out was a series of whistles.

The bird with the green ring on its leg opened its wings and flew up onto the metal rail that ran round the balcony. Then it turned its head and looked expectantly back in his direction. Otto knew immediately what was expected. Maximillian wanted them both to follow him up onto the rail.

But could he actually fly? Tentatively, he spread his wings and immediately discovered that his new body understood perfectly well what to do. He flapped and fluttered and a moment later he was perched on the rail beside Maximillian with Juliet on the other side. Maximillian turned his head and looked at them each in turn. Then he looked ahead at the vast, empty expanse of sky that stretched before them all the way to the northern mountains.

Once again, Otto knew exactly what Maximillian was trying to tell them. In a minute he was going to launch himself out into that blue grey void and sail high above the jagged rooftops of Omustakah. He wanted Otto and Juliet to follow.

Otto had already discovered that he could fly, but it was one thing fluttering from the ground up to the rail of the balcony and quite another trusting his wings to carry him on a long journey. Every human memory he possessed warned him that he would fail, that he would simply plummet to earth like a stone and the life would be smashed from his fragile body. But he was no longer human and there was another part of his mind, the bird part, that assured him he could do it.

Maximillian uttered a harsh cry and took to the air. Otto hesitated for a moment then made up his mind and followed. At exactly the same time, Juliet launched herself from the rail. A moment later all three of them were sailing serenely over the rooftops of Omustakah.

Flying was wonderful. Otto climbed higher and higher, delighting in his new-found ability. From up here the Nevatski horsemen who surrounded the smoking palace were like tiny dots. Moving towards them he could see another great mass of dots – the citizens of Omustakah, clearly determined to fight back. Otto turned away from such matters and gave his attention to the air instead, and to the two birds flying beside him.

The sky, he now realised, was not the great stretch of emptiness and water vapour that he had always imagined. Everywhere it was criss-crossed by pathways, invisible to the human eye, but perfectly clear to his bird senses. Magnetic lines of force that told him where he was in relation to the great, spinning globe beneath him. He circled and swooped and dived for the sheer joy of it.

Another sharp call came from up ahead. Otto turned his head and saw immediately what Maximillian was trying to show him. In the distance was the forest where they had first emerged in Quillipoth. That was where they had to head for. This was no time for acrobatics.

Otto opened his beak and gave an answering cry that meant he understood. Then he beat his wings strongly and settled into a steady pattern that would carry him over the miles without tiring him unnecessarily. Juliet soon followed suit.

Soon they had left Omustakah behind. The air turned cold and below them were the mountains, wrapped in snow. Pine-forests covered the slopes and somewhere among them Otto remembered there was a tiny red flag that Maximillian had stuck in the ground so that they would know how to find their way back home.

As he flew, Otto thought about the change that had come over him. He had not merely taken on the appearance of a bird. He really *was* a bird. And more than that, he felt as if some part of him had always been a bird, always known the exhilaration of flying. It would be hard to give this up again. And for what?

Human beings were such limited creatures, shackled to the earth as if they were made of stone. If they wanted to fly, they had to build great winged engines out of metal, flinging themselves upwards with all the noise and disruption of some monstrous dragon from ancient times. Whereas birds had only to stretch out their wings and take advantage of the mighty power of the wind, always there, forging its currents across the great ocean of air.

Yes, he decided. He was in love with being a bird and he would never go back to being human. When they finally found Maximillian's flag he would tell the other two of his decision. They could resume their former bodies, go back through the portal and take up their old lives again. But he would stay here. The bird part of him would grow and grow until he forgot all about the world he had left behind, all about Otto Spinoza and the flat above the bookshop. He would be wild. And he would be free.

13

THE RED FLAG

Cornelius was all by himself and far from happy about it. In fact he was downright worried. So worried that the fur on his tail was sticking up. He hated it when that happened. It was so very undignified – and dignity was important to Cornelius.

No cat likes to admit that it needs human beings. Of course it will allow itself to be stroked by them, it will even rub round a human's legs and purr at times. But these are only strategies to enable it to get what it wants. Usually food. Or milk. Or cream.

But in their hearts cats are loners. They don't go around in packs like dogs. They don't walk along after human beings desperately trying to win their approval. They look after themselves. They live on their wits. They fall on their feet. They escape by a whisker. And they do it all by themselves.

But what if you've been magically transported to another world and there is absolutely no chance of you getting back to your own world without a human being to reverse the spell? And what if you've lost track of that human being? What if the last time you saw him, he was about to have his head chopped off by a mob of blood-thirsty elementals? What do you do then?

Frankly, Cornelius didn't know. So he was falling back on the advice Maximillian had given them all when they first arrived in Quillipoth. 'If we get separated, meet back here.' But would there be anyone for him to meet?

He had sneaked away from the square where the angry elementals had seized his companions, keeping to the shadows. No one had noticed him. But he hadn't felt good about it. If he'd been a dog, no doubt he would have thrown himself at the elementals in a fury of snarling teeth. He might even have bitten a few throats before being clubbed to the ground. But what good would it have done? There were hundreds of elementals in that square, all baying for blood. No, he'd done the only thing he could. All the same, he felt guilty.

Wet and cold and thoroughly miserable, Cornelius picked his way through the snowy forest above Omustakah, in search of the red flag that Maximillian had planted there. Perhaps it was because he was so preoccupied with his thoughts, that he failed to realise he was being followed.

Keeping a close watch on his progress from behind a huge fir tree was an elemental with loose greyish skin, a very long nose like a trunk, and enormous ears. In his hand he carried an axe with a wickedly sharp blade.

While Cornelius was edging around drifts of snow and frozen puddles, three large black birds were circling in the sky above. Fortunately, birds' eyes are a great deal better equipped than those of humans for picking out small objects on the ground below them. So it didn't take them long to discern a tiny spot of colour amid the bleak, wintry landscape below. Maximillian gave a raucous cry of triumph that was answered by Otto and Juliet and the three birds began their descent.

This was where they would part company,

Otto decided, as the three birds fluttered down to land on the snow-covered ground. The other two would return to their human shapes but he would remain unchanged. He would resist whatever spell Maximillian tried to use upon him. He had to be ready to feel the spell coming. Being a bird was quite different to being a human. He was more aware of the invisible world where magic has its roots. Now he focused on this awareness, the way that a dog pricks up its ears to catch a distant sound. And he felt the spell before it hit him.

To his new bird senses a magic spell was like a cloud of ever-shifting colours drifting in his direction. It looked pretty enough but he knew perfectly well that it was full of pain and that it would turn him back into what he had been before – a two-legged animal that went around destroying the wild places, filling them with its noise and ugliness. He was not going to let that happen to him.

But even as he was filling his mind with resistance he became aware that the bird that had once been Maximillian was thinking something at him. Not in the way that human beings shared thoughts using the slow and clumsy method of words, but in the way that all animals could communicate despite the different sounds they might all choose to make. The bird that had once been Maximillian was using the older language of pictures. It was showing him a picture of an older female human being. It was asking him to remember who this female human being was and what she meant to him.

Otto didn't want to look at the picture. He didn't want to remember. But he had no choice. The memory came flooding back of its own accord. She was his mother. She was sitting on the sofa in an enchanted sleep in the flat above the bookshop. She was waiting for him to return and wake her up.

A great wave of sadness rolled over Otto as he understood that he could not stay a bird no matter how much he wanted to. He would have to go back to being a human. It was his destiny. Reluctantly, he lowered his resistance and the cloud of ever-changing colours engulfed him.

The pain was even worse than last time. Red hot needles stuck themselves into his skin. His head felt as though it were being torn from his body and he struggled to breathe as all the air was sucked out of his chest. The world spun round and round so fast he wanted to be sick. Then everything went black and he felt certain that this time he really was dead.

But a few moments later he opened his eyes to find himself lying on the snow, in his human form once more, sore all over but otherwise unharmed. Beside him were Maximillian and Juliet.

All three of them got to their feet.

'That was a close thing,' Maximillian said. 'Another ten minutes in bird shape and I might have lost you altogether, Otto.'

Juliet was looking all around anxiously. 'Where's Corny?' she said. 'I really hoped he'd be waiting for us here.' She called out his name but there was no response. 'What if something's happened to him?' she said, wandering towards the edge of the clearing and calling out once more.

Suddenly two men stepped out from behind a tree near Juliet. One of them grabbed her, locking his arm round her throat and holding a gun to the side of her head. She screamed as Maximillian and Otto ran towards her.

'That's far enough!' said the other man,

a hugely fat figure who was horribly familiar. 'Don't come any closer.'

'Mr Jones!' Otto said, miserably.

'We meet again,' Mr Jones said. 'Allow me to introduce my colleague Mr Spinks. Mr Spinks is a government magician. Oh yes, we have them. Mr Spinks tracked you down using the whisker that you used to create the simulacrum of your cat. It wasn't easy but Mr Spinks is a very hard worker. He followed the trail all the way to the disused fountain in the grounds of Belsham Manor. Then it was just a question of reverse-engineering your spell. It took time of course but as you can see, it worked. All we had to do next was sit tight near your little red flag and wait for you to turn up. I must say we didn't expect you to arrive in quite the way that you did. A very interesting spell. Mr Spinks seems to think you managed it with the help of a magical ring. So you can start by handing that over right away or the girl gets a bullet in the head.

Mr Jones didn't look like he was joking.

Reluctantly, Maximillian removed the ring from his finger.

'Drop it on the floor and step away

from it,' Mr Jones ordered.

Maximillian did as he was told.

Mr Jones stepped forward, picked up the ring and put it on his finger. 'Now, give me the tablet,' he said.

'You don't understand,' Maximillian replied. 'The information on the tablet is incredibly dangerous. Used wrongly it has the power to destroy the entire world.'

Mr Jones laughed out loud, 'Do you think I don't realise that? My department has been researching the Forbidden Spell for years. The moment we realised what was written on the tablet we made up our minds to remove it from the exhibition ourselves.'

'Except you were beaten to it,' Otto said.

'Exactly. Of course we realised who had taken it and we guessed he was hiding somewhere in Quillipoth, but we needed somebody to come here and get it back for us. And I must say, you've done a remarkably good job.'

'Why do you always have to do everything by force?' Otto said, in an exasperated tone. 'If you'd just asked us, we would have cooperated with your investigation.'

'And risk you keeping the tablet for yourselves?'

'We wouldn't have done that.'

Mr Jones shook his head. 'Maybe not, but in my business we can't afford to take any chances, which is why I'll be deactivating your precious Janusian Portal the moment I get back. So you'd better start getting used to the climate because you're all staying here. Now hand over the tablet before things get messy.'

'Don't give it to him!' Juliet said defiantly.

But out of the corner of his eye, Maximillian had noticed something going on in the trees above them. Keeping his expression completely blank, he nodded. 'You win,' he said.

A few moments earlier, unseen by anyone, Cornelius had arrived at the edge of the clearing and, seeing what was happening, he had climbed quickly and silently up a tree – directly above where Mr Jones was standing.

He was not a heroic cat but he was not a coward either. He knew that this time he could not run away. He had to do something to save his friends. Besides, he had a score of his own to settle with Mr Jones. Just as Maximillian was about to hand over the tablet, Cornelius leapt from the tree, landing with all his claws extended on the top of Mr Spinks' head.

Mr Spinks yelled, dropped the gun, released his hold on Juliet and staggered about, arms flailing as he struggled to pull Cornelius from his head, only succeeding in tripping over a rock and falling backwards into the snow.

Both Otto and Mr Jones made a dive for the fallen gun but it was Otto who got there first. Triumphantly, he stepped backwards pointing it in Mr Jones' direction. 'Looks like the tables are turned,' he said.

'Now, don't be silly, young man,' Mr Jones said, backing away. 'You wouldn't actually want to shoot me, would you? I mean that would be murder and I don't think you're the murderous type.'

'Try me!' Otto said, trying to sound as tough as possible, though inwardly he suspected that Mr Jones might be right. Would he really be able to pull the trigger if he needed to?

Fortunately, the decision was taken out of his hands when a booming voice rang out across the clearing.

'Where is the Ugly One?'

All eyes turned in the direction of the Kabolim's former Master of Music who stood on the edge of the clearing, his axe gripped firmly in one hand, his eyes glinting with menace.

It was Maximillian who spoke first. 'He's not here,' he said.

But the elemental had spotted something gleaming on Mr Jones' finger. The hand that was not holding the axe moved with lightning speed to draw a knife from its sheath at his side. Before anyone had understood what was happening the knife flashed through the air and lodged with a dull thump in Mr Jones' chest.

He stood there for a moment looking utterly bewildered, before crumpling slowly to the ground.

Mr Spinks let out a cry of terror and raced into the woods with the elephantine elemental in hot pursuit.

'This is our chance!' Maximillian cried. 'Everybody ready?'

They nodded.

He paced quickly around the clearing, chanting quietly to himself before making a number of rapid movements with his hands.

Last time he had done this it had seemed to Otto as though he were untying an invisible knot. This time it looked as if the knot was once more being tied.

Then Maximillian raised both hands high in the air and began to chant.

Otto felt the familiar itching begin all over his body. Then the clearing was bathed in light.

A moment later they were back in the garden of Belsham Manor.

14

A New Woman

It was still the middle of the night when they found themselves back in their own world beside the dried-up fountain. Despite all their adventures in Quillipoth, no time had passed at all in the grounds of Belsham Manor. At first Otto and Juliet were so elated to be back home safely, they wanted to jump for joy. But on the way out of the abandoned garden, their excitement quickly gave way to exhaustion as the magical sherbet lemons that Maximillian had given them earlier finally began to wear off.

'I really can't go any further,' Otto complained when they reached the door in the wall that led into the cultivated part of the grounds. 'Why don't we just lie down here and go to sleep?'

'Sounds like a good idea to me,' Juliet said.

But Maximillian forced them to keep going until at last they reached his car, whereupon they practically fell inside and were both sound asleep even before they had driven through the manor gates.

It seemed only a few minutes to Otto before he was being woken up again. 'Leave me alone!' he groaned.

'We're back at the bookshop, Otto,' Maximillian told him.

Otto sat up and looked out the window. 'No, we're not,' he said, grumpily.

'You just can't see it because I disguised it,' Maximillian reminded him. 'You have to stand with your back to it and look over your shoulder, remember.'

'Can't you just take the spell off?' Otto said.

'It'll take too long. I'll do it in the morning. Come on, Otto. Come on, Juliet. You can do it!'

Wearily, they went through the business of walking backwards towards the shop and after a bit of fumbling and a lot of moaning Otto finally turned the key behind his back.

Now that he was home, he remembered his mother. 'You have to take the spell off her!' he told Maximillian.

'Don't worry!' Maximillian assured him. 'That's the very next thing I'm going to do.'

Mrs Spinoza was still sitting wrapped in a blanket on the sofa where they had left her, her eyes closed and a peaceful expression on her face. Maximillian muttered something under his breath then touched her on the forehead. In seconds she opened her eyes and sat up.

'I was having the oddest dream,' she said. 'Something about The Tower of Babel.' She frowned. 'It was a dream, wasn't it?'

She looked at each of them in turn.

'How should we know?' Otto asked with a shrug.

She looked at her watch. 'Good heavens! How on earth did it get so late? Off you go to bed!' she ordered.

'What a good idea!' Otto said.

'I'll come back and see you first thing tomorrow morning,' Maximillian told them. 'I think we all need to have a little talk.'

'What did he mean by that?' Mrs Spinoza asked, after he'd left. 'What does he think we need to talk about?'

'Let's wait until tomorrow to find out,' Otto said with a yawn. 'I really am terribly tired.'

'Me too,' Juliet agreed.

Before long the flat above the bookshop was

silent once more except for the sound of three people and a cat breathing deeply.

The next morning they were all awoken by the door bell announcing Maximillian's return.

'I can't think what's the matter with me,' Mrs Spinoza observed, as she stood in the middle of the kitchen in her dressing gown. 'I don't normally sleep so late.'

'That's what I wanted to talk to you about,' Maximillian told her. 'You see I have a confession to make.'

'Go on.' She regarded him sternly.

'I'm afraid I had to put you in an enchanted sleep.'

'An enchanted sleep!' Mrs Spinoza drew herself up to her full height (which wasn't very tall) and stared indignantly up at Maximillian.

'Shall we have breakfast before we talk about this?' Otto suggested. He was feeling awfully hungry.

'No, we shall not have breakfast,' Mrs Spinoza declared. 'Not until I know exactly what's been going on.'

So they told her. It was a long story and Mrs Spinoza was very cross indeed by the end of it.

Even when Maximillian took the camouflage spell off the shop and offered to put on one to attract customers, she refused to be mollified.

'I've had enough of your spells round here, thank you very much,' she declared.

However, when Maximillian announced his intention of destroying the clay tablet, she defrosted enough to agree with him.

'I should think so, too,' she said.

'But what about the exhibition?' Juliet asked.

Maximillian shook his head. 'There can't be any exhibition,' he said. 'The tablet is far too dangerous to let anyone else see it. We can't risk it getting into the hands of people who would use it as a weapon.'

'Supposing the government start asking questions about Mr Jones' disappearance,' Otto said.

'Then we tell them the truth,' Maximillian replied. 'He was killed by an angry elemental.'

'And if they ask about the tablet?'

'We tell them that somebody destroyed it.'

'But that isn't true,' Juliet pointed out.

'It soon will be,' Maximillian replied.

He left the house then and returned shortly afterwards with a very solid-looking hammer which he had purchased from a local hardware store. Before anyone could try to change his mind he went out into the yard behind the bookshop and smashed the tablet into pieces. Those pieces he smashed into smaller pieces and he kept on until all he had left was a little pile of dust. He swept this up with a dustpan and brush and poured it into an envelope.

A little later, when Mrs Spinoza was downstairs in the bookshop, Juliet said, 'I still feel a bit bad about Ms Gauntlet. Don't you think we should give her the real tooth back?'

'Are you crazy?' Otto replied. 'She's practically psychotic. We'll be lucky if she doesn't attack us with a carving knife.'

Cornelius agreed. 'I was very nearly killed the last time we went to see that woman,' he pointed out.

But once Juliet had made up her mind to do something it was practically impossible to persuade her otherwise, especially if that something was a matter of conscience. Eventually she persuaded the others that it was the right thing to do and, to Otto's surprise, his mother agreed when they went downstairs to discuss it with her.

'Stealing is stealing,' she told them, 'even if it was only a tooth.'

'Just a fragment of tooth, actually,' Otto pointed out.

'Size is not important,' his mother insisted. 'It wasn't yours and you must give it back. But no getting into any other adventures while you're doing it. Promise?'

Otto, Juliet and Maximillian promised.

She looked at Cornelius who had been busy washing himself. He gazed back at her for some time. Finally, he said, 'No self-respecting cat could possibly agree to such a promise. However, you may rest assured that I have not the slightest intention of entering that woman's house again as long as I live.'

So that afternoon they set off once more for Haverstock. To Otto's relief Maximillian's car was back to normal and they sped up the motorway in comfort. All the same, no one was looking forward to reaching their destination. But when they finally arrived outside Ms Gauntlet's house they were in for a surprise.

The house still looked shabby and in need of painting but the litter was gone from the front garden, the lawn had been mowed and there was a basket of flowers hanging beside the front door.

They rang the front door bell and a smartly dressed woman with an air of purposeful efficiency opened the door. It took a moment for Otto to realise that it was Madeleine Gauntlet. She looked as if she had been the subject of a TV makeover.

'Can I help you?' she asked brightly.

It was obvious that she hadn't recognised them but when Maximillian reminded her that they had called before to make some enquiries about Lucas Mendicant she nodded and invited them in. 'The last few weeks have been a bit of a blur, I'm afraid,' she explained as she ushered them into a bright, clean living room in which there was not one single photograph of Lucas Mendicant to be seen. 'You see, I haven't been very well. But I'm quite recovered now. So, please sit down. I'm afraid I can't give you very long, though. I have to leave the house shortly. I've got a job interview.'

Maximillian explained that they just wanted to ask her a few more questions about Lucas Mendicant.

'You know it's the strangest thing,' she said,

as she perched on the edge of a chair facing them, 'but only yesterday I would have been delighted to talk to anyone about Lucas Mendicant. To tell you the truth,' she said, 'I was positively infatuated with the man. Like a woman enchanted.' She shook her head. 'It seems completely absurd now.'

'So you don't feel like that any more?' Otto asked.

'Certainly not,' she said. 'I woke up this morning and suddenly everything seemed different. The first thing I did was phone up Haverstock University and speak to the Dean. He was ever so understanding. Such a nice man. I can't have my old job back of course because Mr Mendicant doesn't work there any more, but he said he was sure they could fix me up with something. So, you see, I really don't have a lot of time to chat.

'Of course,' Maximillian said. 'We understand that and we won't take up any more of your time than necessary. There was just one thing we wanted to ask.'

'What was that?'

'It was about that tooth fragment of Lucas Mendicant's that you kept under your pillow.'

'Oh that!' Ms Gauntlet said scornfully, 'I'm afraid it's in the dustbin. I don't know what was the matter with me, sleeping with that under my pillow. It's so dreadfully embarrassing. Was it terribly important? Because the dustbin men haven't been yet. I suppose you could go through the rubbish if you really want to. I've got some rubber gloves in the kitchen.'

Maximillian smiled reassuringly. 'I don't think that will be necessary,' he said. He got to his feet and the others followed suit.

'So was that it?' Ms Gauntlet said, looking puzzled.

'Yes, thanks,' Maximillian said. 'That was it. We won't waste any more of your time, Ms Gauntlet. You've really been most helpful.'

They left Madeleine standing in her doorway, still looking confused.

'Well that just about sews the whole thing up,' Otto said as they got back in the car.

'Not quite,' Maximillian said. 'There's just one more little task.'

They drove back towards Bridlington Chawley in silence, still a little stunned by the change that had come over Ms Gauntlet. On the way, Maximillian stopped at a motorway service station and bought them all drinks. He even managed to find a saucer of milk for Cornelius. Then they walked along the footbridge over the motorway. Halfway across Maximillian stopped, took out the envelope with the powdered remains of the clay tablet inside and emptied its contents into the wind.

Otto, Juliet and Cornelius looked on in silence.

'I hated doing that,' he said, as they walked back to the car. 'I've spent my whole life learning about magic only to destroy the most powerful magical object that the world has ever seen.'

'Poor Max!' Juliet said sympathetically. 'It was the right thing to do.'

'Never mind,' Otto said. 'Why don't you have a lemon sherbet? I'm sure you'll feel better after that.'

'What a good idea!' Maximillian said with a grin.

THE MAGICAL DETECTIVES

BRIAN KEANEY

OTTO'S WORLD IS ABOUT TO CHANGE FOR EVER...

Otto Spinoza's mother is missing.
A strange man who claims to be a
magical detective offers to help.
But can Otto trust him?

Soon Otto, his friend Juliet and her
cat Cornelius find themselves in a
dangerously weird world where
anything is possible...

978 1 408 30681 9 £5.99 PB

OUT NOW!

Read on for an exclusive extract of
The Magical Detectives...

To look at, there was nothing very remarkable about Otto Spinoza. He was about average height for a boy of twelve. He had very clear blue eyes and floppy brown hair, which he was in the habit of tossing back from his forehead from time to time. His teacher at school thought he was rather quiet, but she concluded that he was merely thoughtful and left it at that.

However, there were at least two things about Otto that *were* very much out of the ordinary. The first was the fact that from as far back as he could remember, Otto had had the feeling that he was different from the other boys and girls in his school; for some reason, which he could not quite put his finger on, he simply did not belong. He didn't talk about this feeling to anyone, because he didn't want to seem rude or stuck-up. But it was always there.

The second unusual thing about Otto was the mystery of his father's death: he had died of a rare tropical disease shortly after Otto was born. So rare was this disease, that no one else in England had ever contracted it, and by the time the hospital realised what was wrong, it was too late to do anything about it. The doctors had been extremely puzzled because even in the jungles of Borneo, where the disease originated, it had only reared its ugly head a few times in the last hundred years. The conclusion they had come to was that Mr Spinoza, who was a bookseller by trade, must have been bitten by an insect that had stowed away in a crate of books he had bought at an auction the week before.

Otto had often wondered why the insect had not bitten anyone else, such as the person who put the books in the crate in the first place, or the auctioneer, but no one seemed to know the answer to this.

Otto and his mother lived in the sleepy little town of Bridlington Chawley, in an apartment above the second-hand bookshop that his mother now ran. It was not the sort of home you see featured in magazines or on television programmes. The furniture was rickety, the carpets threadbare and the rooms all needed a coat of paint. But Otto did not mind all that. He liked living above a bookshop because he loved to read, and there were always plenty of books waiting for his attention.

Otto's mother was a dreadful worrier. When it rained, she worried that the roof might leak, when it was cold she worried that the central heating might break, and when it was warm she worried that it would not last. She worried about her health, and about her weight, about whether or not she was going to be able to pay all the bills. But most of all she worried about Otto, and in particular about what would become of him if anything should happen to her.

'They'll come round sticking their noses in, asking all sorts of questions, that's what they'll do,' she frequently complained. 'Then they'll take you away and put you in a home for orphans. There'll be no one to care for you, no one to look after you. Oh, Otto, I can't bear to think about it!'

At this point she always burst into tears and Otto was obliged to make her a cup of strong tea, and open a packet of biscuits.

Otto's mother had a great fondness for biscuits. They were the only thing that really stopped her worrying for any length of time. It was because of this that Otto was not present when one of the most extraordinary things in the history of Bridlington Chawley took place. She had sent him to the corner shop for a couple of packets of chocolate digestives. So he only discovered what had happened when he returned.

It was the first day of the summer holidays, and all the way to the shop Otto was thinking about what he would do in the weeks to come. Other children in his class went on holiday to exotic places, but there was no chance of that for Otto. Even if they could afford to go away, his mother would be far too worried to contemplate such a trip. Perhaps if his father had been alive, Otto thought to himself, things might have been different.